For those I love.

Evelyn,

With my love,

Dee

xx

CONTENTS

KNIGHTS OF TEMPLE BRUER

By Dee Horne

FACTS

Lincoln is a melting pot filled with an exciting mixture of historical and modern architecture, different cultures and religions, with many old and new stories to be told.

Temple Bruer in Lincolnshire was founded during the late reign of Henry ll (1154-89) and is one of the few Knights Templar sites left in England where ruins remain standing. Its South Tower has survived to this day and is a Grade 1 Listed Building.

The 'Old Religion' is said to have begun 35,000 years ago in Northern Europe.
Shamans were said to have certain powers and were/are in tune with animals.

The foundations of Lincoln Cathedral were first laid in 1072. Bishop Hugh, born around 1140, was said to be filled with kindness, tolerance and had a love for animals.

In the 1630s, a group of Puritans known as The Pilgrim Fathers, left Boston, Lincolnshire to form a new settlement in Massachusetts, USA. They named it after their own hometown.

The County of Lincolnshire has many amazing places to visit!

SISTERS

17 Years Previously ...

A blue Ford Fiesta crept along the curb before halting outside the dilapidated Victorian house. It had clearly been converted into four flats. One of the many old houses, once beautiful and grand, to become lucrative business opportunities for the crude city investors.

Lincoln now boasted highly respected Universities, which meant there was money to be made. For this once small historical city, of little importance to anyone living outside of Lincolnshire, situated in the middle of the most stunning countryside, had suddenly been invaded by students, their professors and families, now all requiring places to sleep, eat, shop, socialize and even worship.

The Fiesta's attractive and smartly dressed occupant switched off her engine, before checking the address that was scribbled down on a note. She studied the house again; the number written on the page said 27C. Although she had noticed the house retained a large driveway, she decided to remain parked out in the street.

Slowly and purposely, stepping out from the warmth and safety of her carriage, the young woman again observed the substantial property before her. While examining its original grandeur, she was drawn to the window of the flat at the top of the right-hand side. She noticed a slight movement from the thick fully drawn drapes. Suddenly, she felt worried ... and surprisingly cold as she shuddered. *She was aware she was being watched.*

Zoe, an elegant woman in her mid-twenties, began walking nervously along the path, leading to the imposing original oak front-door. She was wearing a smart navy-blue knee-length dress with bright red beads, earrings and matching red court-shoes and handbag. Her long, dark, wavy hair was pulled up by two combs on either side of her head, framing her alluring face of soft perfect pale skin, bright blue eyes and full shapely red-painted lips. She now wished she had worn a different style of clothes for this occasion, feeling she was over-dressed.

She noticed the four labelled doorbells, belonging to each flat. 27C was the only one that ceased to have a name written beside it. Having studied it for a few seconds, then inhaling a large in-take of breath, she pressed it ... and waited.

Seconds later, Zoe noticed that the door was unlocked and left slightly ajar. Having nervously pushed it open, she found herself entering an old-fashioned hallway. Her heels made a large echo-ing sound on the cold, original black and white floor tiles.

The walls were a grubby white, as was the ceiling – and the elegant coving had remained. Also, having survived, was a large rose centrepiece, where long pointed crystals from the original chandelier still hung, grasping desperately to the antique pieces of thin wire. Once it would have added luxury and opulence to this grand entrance hall. Nowadays, however, it was wasted; unnoticed as the hall had lost most of its original design, shape and size due to the cheap conversion. It had been reduced to an ugly, neglected entrance, with scruffy modern doors leading to the four inhabited flats.

The door with the crudely painted 'C' was left slightly ajar. Zoe hesitated before slowly opening it and finding herself at the bot-tom of a flight of uncarpeted stairs.

She closed the door behind her and began to ascend the narrow yet steep steps, the heels of her shoes now making a loud *clunking* sound upon the bare wooden boards. The inhabitant would certainly have been pre-warned of her arrival by now!

Zoe could smell the strong, welcoming burning aroma of the sweet incense, drifting through the dry thick air. It felt warming and familiar; she relaxed, just a little.

Once at the top of the stairs, Zoe could see the kitchen straight ahead, but then a woman's recognisable voice called from behind her.

She turned to see the living-room door being held open at the other end of the hall,

"Zoe! Come this way!"

With the door being held fully open now, Zoe locked eyes with the face she had not seen in a few years. She hardly recognised her old friend; Rose looked thinner and much older than Zoe remembered.

She attempted to hide her shock as she walked towards where Rose was eagerly waiting.

Once inside the large living-room, Rose hastily shut the door and threw her arms around Zoe.

"It is so good to see you again," she said. "Thank you for coming so quickly. I wasn't sure whether you would come at all!"

Zoe remained calm and thoughtful.

"You are aware that I can no longer associate with anyone from our Coven, from my past? I do not practise ... our *craft*, anymore."

"Yes, I know," Rose acknowledged solemnly. "I appreciate you have risked a lot by agreeing to see me like this. Please come and sit down."

Rose showed her to an old, comfy and brightly patterned armchair then pulled up another wooden chair for herself to sit opposite. She lifted the china pot, which was placed beside a small pile of official documents on the coffee table between them. She began pouring a red coloured herbal tea into two matching delicate cups with saucers and then handed one of them to Zoe. Zoe took an appreciative sniff, followed by a small sip of the hot steaming fluid.

"Oh, I haven't tasted this for a while, thank you," she said, replacing the china back onto the table. Then she asked the question that had been burning-up inside of her, ever-since receiving the note. "So, why did you contact me, Rose?"

The joy upon Rose's face from having seen her dear old friend again, now faded and she appeared pale and ill.

"I am frightened," she began, "so very fearful, for I did something terrible. I didn't mean to ... you understand? I didn't realise, you see. He never told me that he was loved by *her*. I would never have done it ... if I had only known ... I wouldn't have, would I? But her fury is great! She wishes to punish me! She will find me; it is only a matter of time now - I know she will find me!"

Desperately trying to make sense of Rose's jumbled and hysterical words and becoming more confused by the second, Zoe gently interrupted.

"Please," she said, "just take your time. Now you say you've done something terrible, yet the dear Rose I remember, would never hurt a fly. So, please take a deep breathe, from the beginning, tell me what you think you have done that is causing you such distress."

Rose put her head in her hands for a few seconds, then looking up and staring into Zoe's eyes, almost searching them for an instant answer to her problems, she began.

"It was a couple of years ago, I was attending a Sabbat with the Brothers and Sisters from our own Coven and others. Before taking part in one of the rituals for the Solace, I met a man. He was called Dreamer."

Rose's eyes began to fill with tears, yet a faint smile curled the ends of her dry cracked lips, "He was so quirky and interesting. He was tall with dark, almond coloured skin, bright blue eyes and he wore his hair in long brown and blonde plaited dread-locks. We sat together, just talking, for hours. He confided in me that he was unhappy because he was being forced to do something that he didn't want to do. Of course, I asked him what it was, but he said that it was safer for me not to know and for him to go along with it rather than to refuse. He said that the hours he had spent with me were the happiest he could ever remember. Later, evening approached, and we made love under the stars."

Suddenly, a dark expression appeared across her face; sadness and fear replaced the gentle smile.

Rose continued, "It was later that night, when we had re-joined the members of our own Covens, when Grace, as Priestess led a fertility ritual. *But it was for herself!* Then I saw *him*, entering the Circle! I could not believe what I was seeing! I was part of the Circle, with ten others; cloaked and chanting when he walked straight passed me, took her hand and led her out of the Circle and then into the forest. I fear she might have noticed my reaction."

Again, Zoe interrupted. "You were not to know, Rose. It was not your fault; he should have told you."

Rose stared downwards, at the old tattered rug upon the other-wise, bare wooden floorboards,

"Do you remember how concerned we all became, the months leading up to the time that you left us? How dark, cold and cruel Grace was becoming? You had noticed it too; I know you had!"

Zoe nodded. "I have been gone over three years now. Is she still … experimenting … with the … *darker side*?"

Rose answered fearfully, "She just became worse. Our mother

passed-away around the same time and I hoped that her parting might make us closer. It did not. She grew even more conceited, egotistic, cruel and vindictive. She made our Coven take part in certain rituals … frightening ones! I can tell you, Zoe, we were petrified! Then Tina and Liz, remember them? Such sweet and giggly girls. Well, they suggested that a few of us start meeting together, without Grace. She turned up one night, uninvited and she was furious. She called us 'betrayers' and warned us that we would soon *know the extent of her powers'*, that *'we had no idea of who we were dealing with'* and that *'from now on, we would do exactly as she said or face the consequences'*. We all left the gathering feeling terrified that night and within the week, Tina and Liz, who had vehemently opposed her, lo and behold, were dead, a virus apparently."

Zoe was silent, feeling numb inside as the realisation of her original doubts and fears, buried deep beneath the layers of her new life, were correct and now devastatingly affecting the lives of others, here in her present.

Rose took a sip of tea then continued with her story.

"As the weeks following the ritual passed, she became angrier and frustrated; she wasn't pregnant. Then one day she called me to go to her house, to assist her in creating a powerful love potion. I did what I had to do, but as I was leaving her house, Dreamer was walking up the path. He seemed so pleased to see me and took hold of my hand. He said that he was sorry and that he was about to do everything he could so we could be together. He said he could talk to Grace and make her understand. At that moment, I saw *her* watching us from the window. Even from a distance, I could see the fury in her eyes – I *felt* it too. I begged him not to go inside, not to enter the house but to leave with me straight away. But he said I should trust him."

"Did you see him again?" Zoe enquired.

"No, I haven't seen him since that day. I rushed home, packed a few belongings and have been hiding from her ever since. Fortunately, the money my mother left me in her will has enabled me to live a private life. I don't go out much."

"I see," Zoe was sadly shaking her head.

Rose smiled, "It has not been so bad. The worst part is not being able to go to the forest whenever the mood takes me; to wander barefoot and feel the ground beneath my feet, the movement and life of the trees and the breeze upon my face. But the good side is that I have learned that I was blessed with stronger gifts and powers than I had ever realised." She laughed, momentarily lighter, showing-off as her chair slid slowly, silently and effortlessly across the room, then returned to its original place.

Rose pulled a funny face, "See," she said, "I can do lots of silly and useless stuff like that now. Not much good against a *dark witch* though, is it?"

"No, it isn't," Zoe replied, unimpressed by this extraordinary spectacle. Reaching out, she put her hand upon the now trembling arm of her old and dear friend, "Rose, your abilities are something you should never question. Before *she* came along and you ... allowed her to take *your* rightful position as our High Priestess, you were without doubt, the most inspirational and powerful woman any of us had ever known. You have the *gifts*, the capabilities to have made a stand against her, why didn't you?"

Rose appeared sad and broken, "I had lost our mother and not much else mattered to me at that time. My sister wanted to be the High Priestess and I wanted the unrest she was causing within the Coven to stop. Now, of course, I know I made a terrible decision – I made a huge mistake and it has cost the lives and freedom of many others. Our people have been forced to commit wrongs knowing that the Book says, 'Whatever they have done, will come back thrice multiplied, in amplified repercussion.' It was my mistake, I let it happen, yet so many others are paying for it."

"I can help you, Rose," Zoe announced confidently, "My husband has contacts all over the world. We can make you disappear; unfortunately, Missionaries and Charity Workers go missing in remote and hostile countries every year, never to be seen or heard of again."

Rose suddenly sat up straight in her chair, her problems put on hold as her questioning mind required some long-awaited answers. "Yes! How is that husband of yours? Harry ... no, Howard, wasn't it? You never did get the chance to tell me how you met him."

Zoe smiled, "Oh yes, my wonderful Howard. Well, do you remember that night we had a *ritual* in Jameson's Field, behind the old church where that miserable Scottish Vicar came back unexpectedly?"

Rose laughed, "Oh my goodness, do I?! I had to run all the way home with nothing but my cloak on! My car was parked on the other side of the road, I could hear the police sirens and see the blue flashing lights getting nearer. A couple of our lot got arrested that night, as I recall, but all the charges were dropped. You weren't one of them, were you?"

"I could have been," Zoe replied. "I had taken off my robe before I entered the Circle. Due to the excitement of the raid, I panicked and was disorientated – I could not remember where I had left it! Anyway, I was huddled behind one of the tombstones in the graveyard and I could hear the Vicar speaking to a younger man who was about to receive his priesthood in the coming weeks. He was telling him that *the area had a serious problem with 'Devil Worshippers'* and that he *must keep an eye out for any signs of it.* Then he instructed the younger man, Howard, to take a walk around the graveyard and check for anyone who might have been hiding there, whilst he went to speak with the arriving Police Officers.

Suddenly I was aware of someone standing over me, lightly tapping my naked shoulder. Horrified, I looked up to find Howard looking down at me and holding my robe in his other hand. He smiled and asked, "Are you missing this, by any chance? You must be freezing!" He wrapped the cloak around me then led me to his car, close by. He told me to wait for him inside it then returned a few minutes later. I remember him putting the heater on full-blast and he drove me home. I fell in love with him that night and he felt the same about me. We saw one another secretly for a few weeks until I had to make a tough decision. So, I did the only thing I could – I moved out of my mother's home and became the wife of a Christian Preacher!"

Both women laughed. Then came a short awkward silence, before … "Are you happy, Zoe? I mean, are you fulfilled?"

The reply came easily and without hesitation. "Yes! Howard is remarkable. I consider myself to be truly blessed, I am privileged to be sharing my life with such an amazing man. Our destinies were inter-twined, I know this beyond any doubt."

Still, Rose was not satisfied, "If I recall correctly, you had a few impressive *gifts* of your own. Are you expecting me to believe that you don't practise at all now?"

"That is correct. If it ever came to light that Howard was married to … well … a witch. I think his congregation might dwindle a bit, don't you!"

"Those bloody Christians," Rose joked, "Always out to spoil our fun and we had never even heard of The Devil until *they* came along!"

At that moment, a soft cry could be heard coming from the next room. Zoe looked to Rose for an explanation. However, Rose quickly left the room, returning seconds later, holding a small child wrapped in a blanket. She returned to her chair, snuggling the small toddler who had olive skin, the deepest blue eyes, plump, flushed cheeks and dark sweaty curls sprawled across her cute damp face. On noticing the stranger seated opposite (a rare sight) she clung to her mother, frowning back at Zoe.

"It is alright, Leah," Rose assured her daughter, "This is our friend, Zoe. She won't hurt us; she is kind and will protect you." The child appeared to relax.

"She is beautiful." Zoe said thoughtfully. "I assume she is the reason you are hiding?"

"Yes."

"Does she have any *abilities*, was she born with *gifts?*"

"It appears she was," replied Rose.

"Does her father, know about her?"

Rose hesitated before answering, "I told you, I never saw him again after that day. I could not risk trying to find him – if Grace ever found out about Leah, the daughter I created out of love with Dreamer, I believe she would be capable of anything."

Rose knew the time had come for her to confront Zoe, the only person in the world she could trust, with the favour she must ask.

"Zoe, my dear friend, I need you to take Leah away with you today. Find her a safe home, somewhere she will never be found. A Christian family, maybe, where she is less likely to ever become aware of her *gifts*. Here are her papers, but you could find her a new identity in a different area or country if you wish. Please Zoe, will you do this for me? For Leah?"

Staring down at the papers which had just been thrust into her hands, Zoe was in total shock and disbelief of the situation.

"Do you really believe that your own sister could hurt you and your daughter, her own blood?" Zoe could not comprehend such a thought.

Suddenly, this heated moment was brought to an abrupt end as the infant began to struggle hysterically in her mother's arms. She cried and screamed, then ... she stopped. She became silent and still, as if she were listening or waiting for a certain imminent sound.

From the silence came a tap on the front door downstairs. "Did you close and lock the door when you came in?" Rose whispered.

"Yes, I think I did," Zoe replied tensely, "Are you expecting anyone else?"

"No."

All three souls in the room, listened silently. The knock came again, harder this time.

Zoe quickly dropped the papers into her bag as Rose stood and then placed Leah into her arms.

"Take her into the bedroom, just until I know who is at the door," Rose's voice was shaking.

Zoe was surprised and extremely relieved when the little girl did not struggle or make a murmur, having been handed over to, until this day, a stranger.

Zoe followed Rose out of the room but for some unknown reason, walked past the bedroom door and stairs, continuing to the kitchen at the far end of the hall. She hid behind the open door, watching nervously through the crack as Rose stepped slowly down the stairs and opened the front-door.

Zoe immediately recognised the voice of the new visitor.

"A nice place you have found for yourself, dear sister. I have waited a long time to give you this, my sweet, *loyal* sibling." *It was her! It was Grace, Rose's younger sister!*

To Zoe's utter disbelief and despair, she watched Grace cup her hands, drawing them close to her mouth and then blow a purple dust into the terrified face of her unsuspecting sister.

Seconds passed as the two women stared into the others' eyes. Rose suddenly took one last deep and difficult breath before collapsing backwards onto the stairs. Her body creating a deliberate barrier of inconvenience to Grace, allowing Zoe precious seconds to plan her next move. She knew she would need to act without hesitation before the child in her arms made a sound.

Scanning the kitchen, to Zoe's relief, there was a back door leading out to a roof garden. Holding on to the heavy toddler was difficult but she managed to quietly open the door, then close it behind them.

As she had suspected, there was a fire escape with steps leading down into the back garden. Frantically trying to avoid her shoes from making a sound on the old iron spiral Victorian staircase, Zoe carried Leah down to the garden, around to the side entrance, then waited behind the wall where she could see her car parked out in the street. She could feel her heart beating heavily in her chest, her arms and shoulders were now in excruciating pain from holding the silent child.

A sudden loud bang, coming from the flat above, caused both Zoe and Leah to jump out of their skin. Black smoke was pouring out of the broken windows. It was then that Zoe saw Grace walking calmly out from the front entrance of the house, to her car which was parked on the driveway.

With the sound of Emergency Rescue Vehicles, fast approaching the scene, Zoe waited for the car to reverse out onto the street and then drive away at a normal speed. With thick smoke invading their lungs, but also masking their escape, Zoe was able to carry Leah to the safety of her own waiting car, unnoticed. Chaos ensued as the blue Fiesta drove away, carrying its unique and precious passengers far from the current danger.

17 Years Later …

The 1960's semi-detached house in Leigh-on-Sea, Essex was dark and still when Pam was suddenly awoken by the familiar sounds of Leah having another bad dream. So as not to disturb William, her husband, she carefully crept from their bed and tip-toed out of their bedroom, across the landing and into Leah's room.

As always, when having one of her nightmares, Leah was breathing heavily, beats of sweat run down her face and her long brown hair had formed shorter damp curls. She was tossing and turning, as Pam knelt by her bedside, just as she has done since Leah had turned the age of twelve and these *nightmares* had first begun.

"There, there, my darling girl. That is enough now. Leave whatever awful place you are in and come home. Think of nice things, Leah." Pam continued stroking her precious daughter's forehead, attempting to calm her, "Think of your music, of the beautiful songs you write. You will be enrolling at the local university soon, making lots of new and exciting friends. We all have so much to look forward to, Leah. Please, please wake up, Darling. Come back to me."

Leah's breathing became less erratic. The sound of Pam's voice was her medicine. She was soon still, having returned to her *safe place*. Pam sighed a deep sigh of relief; there should not be another *episode* for at least another few weeks. Although, worryingly, both Pam and William had noticed how they had recently become more frequent.

On returning to her warm bed, Pam snuggled into her husband who was awake. "Is she alright now?" William was concerned.

"Yes, I think so. She won't even remember it in the morning."

"You are a wonderful mother and she is lucky to have you," William whispered.

Pam smiled, hugged her dear spouse of forty-five years, then replied, "She is lucky to have **you** and so am I."

A Few Months Later ...

Leah was sat at the family dining-room table alone, in the dim, empty and silent house. Today was her birthday, so she had gone into her father's office, somewhere she would normally have never entered without William's permission. She knew where he kept the Communion Wine and located the key to the cabinet on his desk. The wine bottles were lined-up into two rows and she took three bottles. That morning, for it was only the wee early hours of her birthday, she intended to get drunk, for the very first time in her life.

On returning to the dining-room and sitting down at the table with her glass and wine bottles, she had looked around the room, adorned with family photographs. The three faces were always smiling – *oh, she would give anything to go back in time, to those wonderful days, when her parents were still alive and well.*

Leah spent the rest of the day feeling sick and ill although only managing to swallow two bottles of the wine. She had not eaten a proper meal in weeks nor attempted to go shopping. According to the news reports, people were queuing at the supermarkets anyway and she did not feel up to doing that.

When the paramedics had taken her parents away on that hellish evening in late March, one of them had warned her not to leave the house for at least two weeks – and it had been almost a month since. She had had difficulty arranging their funerals due to the government restrictions and nothing had felt real anymore. Even the following Christmas had come and passed without her realising.

The following morning, Leah rose from her bed, still wearing the same clothes she had worn all weekend. On entering the dining room, she noticed the last bottle of wine that she had not managed to drink. Memories of how ill she had felt the previous day caused her to feel extremely nauseous, so she quickly picked it up and walked through to William's office to return it.

As Leah slid the bottle back into the cabinet from whence it came, she noticed a small old-fashioned biscuit tin hidden beneath a few papers and Church documents on the bottom shelf. Without knowing why, she picked it up and carried it over to William's desk then sat down in his chair.

Leah's heart missed a beat as she opened the tin and took out an envelope. On opening it she found it contained a birth certificate and a woman's ante-natal book containing the dates of a baby's vaccinations. The shock of seeing her own Christian name and her date of birth stunned her – she felt she could not breathe. *Her beloved parents had never told her that she was adopted.*

With emotions exploding inside her head, for the first time since that terrible day – she cried. She cried for herself, for her two precious and wonderful parents, Pam and William and she cried for the unfamiliar name on her birth certificate, her biological mother, Rose – probably once a scared young single mother living alone in Lincoln, as the father was stated as … *unknown.*

PROTECTORS

Lincoln - The Present

T he attractive middle-aged man with brown hair and strikingly green eyes grabbed his wife's arm, preventing her from a fall.

"I cease to understand why you choose to wear these ridiculously dangerous high heels, Darling," he said.

"Oh Howard, I have been wearing high heels for the whole of my adult life, I am not going to just suddenly stop, am I!"

"Well, you are getting older now, my dear ... and ..."

The dead silence and the sudden tense air around him, alerted Howard to the fact that he had, once again, truly put his foot right in it! He sensibly decided to now keep quiet and hoped dearly that Zoe might do the same.

Zoe, now in her mid-forties, as attractive and elegant as always, had no intention of admitting to her *annoyingly usually right* husband, that her beloved black shiny boots had been crippling her for the past few hours. So, walking to their car, parked in the carpark of The Forum, she was feeling particularly tired and irritable.

The meeting that Zoe and Howard had been attending was scheduled to last an hour however, it had gone on ... and on ... for almost three. They and the other eight Committee Members, five attending in person and three virtually, all with opinions and different points of view, had finally come to amicable decisions concerning the way forward for the new running of the Food Bank and the date of the next Christmas Social.

Zoe hated these meetings, yet never ceased to be impressed at her husband's gifts for calming tempers, building metaphorical bridges and always keeping a cool head, especially when she and others had utterly lost theirs. She had learned early in their marriage, that being the wife of a 'Man of the Cloth' meant conducting herself impeccably and this would always be a challenge for her. Howard was forever kindly reminding her that people like Mr Ahuja, Mr and Mrs Tilley, Mrs Kenyatta, Mr Chen, Miss Jackson and Mr and Mrs Padanowski were the backbone of The Forum, and that their *commitment and enthusiasm* should be encouraged and appreciated. She knew it was true, however, she had endured enough of their *commitment and enthusiasm* this evening and could quite happily have strangled the lot of them!

Once the Members had said their farewells, Zoe began clearing the tea and coffee mugs onto a tray, Howard held the door open for her and she headed down the stairs towards the kitchen.

Howard walked across the hallway and opened a coded door leading to another staircase. At the top of these stairs was another coded door. He opened it and was greeted by Taylor, his nephew.

 "Hi Howard! I guess you are running late too?" he said, looking up at the clock on the wall.

The room was the entire length and width of the building, resembling a sports hall but with no natural sunlight or windows. There were mirrors all around the walls and a surprisingly high ceiling.

As Howard stood talking to his nephew, a group of men and women, aged in their mid-twenties, continued practising a form of Martial Arts. Dressed in the same black tight clothing, their skills and capabilities were incredible.

Suddenly, a loud chastening voice, coming from Jaz, the groups' instructor, hit their unsuspecting eardrums like a bolt from the blue. Her Chinese ancestry had blessed her with a strikingly attractive face, petite body and straight shiny hair, which was a shocking colour of vibrant green and matched her unusual green eyes.

Her loud, crisp voice bellowed, "No! No, Gemma, you are doing it again! Stephen could have been taken out from behind! What is wrong with you tonight?"

Clearly Jaz was frustrated with her student, who appeared discouraged and humiliated.

Gemma's shoulder-length, red, wavy hair, was wet from sweat. She had pale freckly skin with deep hazel brown eyes and was stunningly physically beautiful. She spoke with an American accent, having been born in Springfield, Massachusetts.

"I'm sorry! I am sorry, Jaz! I'm trying, I really am!"

"Yes, you bloody-well are!" Jaz rebuked, wiping the small drizzle of sweat from her own forehead.

At that moment, Stephen, a powerful-looking man with black skin and a large muscular physique stepped forward and spoke in his deep tranquil voice.

"We all respect the fact that you are trying hard, Gemma, but you've done hundreds of manoeuvres more challenging than this one?" he questioned.

"I guess I could do with a little more instruction tonight," Gemma responded awkwardly.

Howard interrupted, "Hello and goodbye everyone! I will be off now. Don't forget to lock-up after yourselves."

The group of six acknowledged Howard as he left, Taylor closed the door after him.

Howard felt an immense sense of pride; *these young people were indeed extraordinary.*

Zoe had been waiting for Howard at the foot of the stairs, "Everything okay?" she enquired.

"Jaz has them practising an intricate manoeuvre," he said, "but Gemma is struggling with it for some reason. She usually picks these things up really well."

"I tell you," admitted Zoe, "I would not want to be in Gemma's shoes tonight."

"No, and I wouldn't want to be in those uncomfortable looking *tortures* either!" he responded, looking down at her boots while finding himself amusing.

"Home!" she ordered.

With a smile Howard turned and headed towards the Main Hall while Zoe stood at the front entrance. The ground floor of The Forum was designed with the stairs at the front of the building, leading up to meeting rooms, a door which led to the gallery seating for the Main Hall below and the door concealing the staircase to the private sequestered top floor.

On the ground floor, having passed the small café area, with its drink and food vending machines along one of the walls, a small kitchen on the other side and small tables with sensibly placed seating, Howard reached the large impressive old oak door to the Main Hall. Just a couple of hours previously, the whole building had been in use; with various meetings, classes and a band practise all taking advantage of this inclusive and re-markable building, within a mile of Lincoln City Centre. Even the land acquired outside boasted good spaces for the various sports and activities held there. The carpark was adequate for the ever-growing numbers of members, joining-up to partici-pate in the fun, education and support of this unique place.

Once Howard had checked that the Main Hall was empty and the lights were switched off, he headed back to where Zoe was eagerly awaiting his return. Together they stepped out into the chilly night air.

There were just six cars and two motorcycles left in the dimly lit carpark. Zoe had her mind fixated on reaching their car, turning the heater on full and getting home to prepare their pot of tea, to have with their usual couple of chocolate biscuits before retiring to bed. They had just reached their car when she almost stumbled; the soles of her feet and sore toes were now hurting so badly, but Howard was there to save her, as always.

Zoe was looking down at her feet when she was suddenly aware of Howard's hand on her back.

"Oh dear," she heard him sigh, "This isn't good." She felt sick and dizzy as Howard put a protective arm around her and began slowly guiding her backwards.

Suddenly, an eery moment of silence was followed by a loud unexpected CRASH! To their utter shock and horror, someone, or something, had flung themselves through the air, landing on the bonnet of their car directly in front of them.

The security lights from the building automatically switched on revealing the terrifying silhouette. He was a tall, dishevelled character with no hair and protruding teeth. He had large round ball-like eyes and distended ears. His long spindly legs with massive boat-like feet were positioned apart and slightly bent. In one of his dirty cumbersome hands, he held a large razor-edged knife. The traumatised couple clung to each other knowing this *creature* was preparing to pounce at any second. This fiend was well-enough positioned and equipped to kill at least one of them before they had time to even attempt to turn and run, and he knew it, because he began to laugh. It was a terrorizing high-pitched, almost childlike cackle.

To their despair, Howard and Zoe watched, almost in slow motion, as the creature bent his knees lower, preparing to spring and ascend through the air towards his targets. It was obviously clear to see from the cruel look in his eyes, that his intentions were violent.

However, at the precise second that the aggressor elevated his feet from the bonnet and launched himself high into the air, he was utterly shocked and unprepared to be suddenly blocked by a solid wall of pure human muscle. For he had just impacted the broad rigid chest of Stephen, who seemed to have appeared from out of nowhere.

The incensed creature found himself descending backwards, landing abruptly and smashing into a heap onto the hard ground. However, without showing any indication of discomfort, this demon arose from his severe fall completely unshaken. Within seconds, he was back onto his feet still clenching hold of the deadly knife and totally prepared for the challenge ahead.

He was not, however, prepared for the following turn of events. For suddenly, he beheld a sight which caused him to question his own usually perfect vision. Having closed his eyes for a moment, then rubbing them coarsely with his filthy fists, he asked himself whether he was dreaming, or was this unexpected yet arguably impressive spectacle before him, real?

Striding boldly towards him were three young male mortals, all dressed in dark military-looking coats with high collars. The metallic material from which they were made, seemed to glisten and sparkle with the wearers' movements. (He knew of this miraculous fabric of course, but how on Earth did *they*?) In their shimmering, gloved hands were held elegant thin swords. Their appearance was fearsome and intimidating.

The three warriors stopped and stared at their opponent from just a few paces away. Stephen was standing in between the other two. On his left was Taylor, a handsome young man with a cheeky boyish face, short brown hair and remarkably green eyes. On his right stood Mac, dashingly attractive with short thick curly blonde hair and deep blue eyes.

The fiend studied them for a moment before sniggering, "Are you *really* here to oppose *me*?" Mockingly, he then continued, "Your pretty little coats of armour and your pathetic trivial shiny swords, are not a match for me!" His voice was becoming louder and increasingly hysterical as he screeched, "You ridiculous mortal fools! You three *dare* to challenge me?"

At that moment, as if on cue, from the direction immediately behind the arrogant creature came a soft well-spoken female voice, "Well, *sweetie*, of course they wouldn't *dare* challenge you, I mean, not on their own, they wouldn't – would you, boys?"

Howard chose this opportunity to grab Zoe's hand, give her *the nod* and together they ran back to the safety of The Forum, unnoticed by their attacker.

The intrigued demon turned his weird head around, without moving his shoulders or one other part of his body. He was pleasantly surprised to see three beautiful young women, also adorned in the same pewter coats, armed with equally offensive weapons and staring provocatively straight back at him. They too were positioned in an aggressive stance, in a lined formation and stood a few paces behind him.

The demon studied each woman pleasingly. On the left of the three female mortals he saw the one who had just spoken, Shania - with long golden hair and blue eyes. Next, he turned his head slightly to one side, appreciating the *unique one* in the middle, Jaz, with her green hair and eyes. But then the one on the other side of her, Gemma - with hair like fire, spoke in an American accent.

"Yeah, absolutely! These guys cannot go around keeping all the fun for themselves now, can they?"

He was bewildered by their nerve and overconfidence, especially when Jaz then added, "What's the matter? You look like you have just seen a ghost! Well, welcome to the Twenty-First Century where we can, once again, kick yours, and your friends' asses, back to where you all belong!"

Jaz lifted her sword high above her head then pointed it at her enemy – the others did the same. Everything they had been preparing, studying and training for, would be put to the first real test, this very night.

The following few minutes were a mixture of perfectly positioned attack and defensive manoeuvres against an enemy of mighty strength, cunning, rage and ferocity. Having superhuman capabilities, he led the dark-coated warriors into an awesome battle.

Though also skilled and defiant, it was becoming evident that their elaborate and expert swordplay were not a match for this demon's strength and speed. If it had not been for the protection of their mystical coats, deflecting the constant knife jabs and thrusts, they all surely would have been dead within the first minute of the ferocious battle starting. One by one, they were each hurled through the air, landing skilfully, then bravely and immediately, returning to combat.

Soon, the courageous, young *New-Age Knights* were about to receive a lucky break …

Stephen suddenly launched himself from the roof of the nearest car, being Taylor's. Flying through the air, he forcefully landed on his unsuspecting opponent. Both went tumbling to the ground. The creature was instantly pinned down onto his back by Mac and Shania, as Gemma swung her legs either side of his torso and sat on his chest. He was about to free himself when the tantalizingly seducing fire-haired girl spoke to him. He knew he could free himself whenever he chose, so he decided to enjoy himself a little.

"Having fun, *handsome*?" she purred.

He giggled excitedly, "Oh yes, I am!" Screeching sarcastically,

"Thank you for asking!"

Suddenly, he noticed that Stephen had crouched down beside his head. Stephen then spoke calmly, in his deep smooth tone, "If we were to free you tonight and demand that you return to whence you came, what would you do?"

The demon stopped his childish giggling and turned his gruesome head, looking directly into Stephen's dark eyes. His voice vibrated with venomous hatred, "Tonight, all of you, your Master and *his witch* will die." Now he looked back at Gemma, "But I'll be leaving you until last, *poppet*." He winked an eye and gave her the ugliest of smiles, causing Gemma to almost gag.

Stephen responded immediately, as the others knew he would, him being so protective of his wife. "Wrong answer!" he said, taking a small silver pistol from a fold within his coat and firing it directly into the demon's brain.

The tiny bullet made a small hole, which miraculously began to heal immediately. So, Stephen fired it again, this time into the heart area. The creature closed his eyes and turned his head. He was enjoying playing with their emotions and reactions.

After a few silent, hopeful seconds, he opened one eye and joked, "Ouch?"

Next Taylor appeared, holding an elaborately jewelled dagger, he ruthlessly plunged it into the same area. His victim groaned and closed his eyes.

He played with them for another moment, '*The fools think they've won!*' he thought to himself. He opened his eyes and began laughing, then …

Enough was enough, he had had his fun, now it was time for them all to die! But just as he was about to rise, he realised that the knife had actually pinned him to the ground.

To this demon's surprise, Jaz was now sitting on top of him, glaring down at him, having swiftly replaced Gemma. He noticed the thin dazzling golden chain in her hands. He stopped laughing, intrigued but not too concerned. Without warning, his arms were viciously and violently heaved upwards by Taylor and Mac, while Shania withdrew the dagger pinning him down. As his chest was lifted slightly off the ground, Jaz only needed that split second to swiftly slip the chain under his body, then around his abruptly lowered arms. She hastily tied, and then held the two ends of this mysterious chain together in her small dainty hands.

Jaz began instructing the others. "Okay," she began, "We don't know how long this will hold him for, so we must move quickly. Taylor, we will use your car to get him to the *sacred ground*, so go and start the engine!"

Taylor stared back at her indignantly. "But it has already got a bloody great dent in it tonight, from old *Bigfoot* here! Why have we got to use mine?"

Jaz was in no mood for confrontation. "Do it!" she yelled, as Taylor appeared to look scared for the first time this evening. Stephen, Mac and Shania exchanged small smiling glances as Taylor quickly and sensibly, did as he was told.

The demon had begun choking, his bulging eyes were turning red and protruding from their sockets. His face had turned completely grey while black *goo* trickled from his mouth. He was paralyzed, though totally aware of what was happening around him and able to hear and understand the words spoken. He was stunned and confused; he had never been taken down in battle before!

What power has this mystical chain that was binding him, making him utterly helpless? His next thought was of his Master who would not tolerate his failure! He began shaking more violently. *He must free himself, destroy these New Knights and their Leader,* suddenly realising that ...

the Leader had run back inside the protected walls of The Forum, with his witch!

Taylor had the car waiting beside them all now. Gemma assisted Jaz to stand the beast onto his feet, almost allowing him an opportunity to escape, as the chain nearly slipped through Gemma's fingers. With the link momentarily broken, a desperate short struggle ensued as he attempted to break free from his confinement. However, he was weak, and Jaz was too quick reacting to have ever allowed him to regain his freedom.

Maybe he would get another opportunity – he must be ready!

The trembling body was manipulated into the backseat of Taylor's car. Shania placed herself one side of their captive, Jaz the other - she held on tightly to the chain, not removing her eyes from his; attempting to anticipate his every thought and movement.

The demon suddenly remembered her words – *we don't know how long this will hold him for … must get him to sacred ground …*

Maybe this powerful piece of weaponry is not as perfect as they believe! *He would be ready for any chance of escape!*

Taylor drove quickly but skilfully along the dark country lanes. Mac sat in the front passenger seat, constantly monitoring their prisoner in the mirror. He made a call to *someone* who was to meet them.

Stephen and Gemma were escorting the car on their motorcycles.

Soon, the car came to an abrupt halt. Taylor and Mac leapt out from the front and flung open the back doors. Stephen and Gemma pulled up beside them.

In the darkness, the demon peered around at the farm buildings and equipment. He could hear a couple of dogs barking, and a horse neighing excitedly from a nearby field.

Now he was carried through an iron gate, into a small field where a ruin stood.

Oh no! Not this place! How did they know to bring him here? He

must break free before …

The demon had immediately recognised the remains of the old Templar Knights Place of Worship and their Training Camp – Temple Bruer. The restraining young knights felt the demon panic as the reality and seriousness of the situation had become apparent. He suddenly made a high-pitched squealing sound, like a wild dog calling for support from the rest of the pack – but no help came. He was carried up the unmistakable ancient stone steps and the large wooden door was opened by an elderly man who had been expecting their imminent arrival.

The old man, in his ninety-fourth year was remarkably spritely; tall and lean with a little remaining grey hair and bushy eyebrows. His pyjama bottoms had been tucked inside his muddy Wellington boots and he was wearing a thick waxed canvas jacket and a warm knitted scarf. His skin was wrinkled and worn though his eyes were as twinkly as a new bright star.

Inside the towering walls of the old Temple were a pile of large stone blocks in one corner and an ancient knight's casket lid in another. They were barely visible, with just a simple column of moonlight creeping in through the small high window. The demon was placed in the centre and his captors slowly withdrew. The chain released itself, making a clinking sound as it dropped onto the cold hard floor. He fell to his knees, knowing he had failed; there was no escape now.

Looking around the circle of young knights, he wondered, *who are you? How have you acquired the old knowledge? And … what will my Master do now?*

Suddenly, Stephen fired the small pistol once more. This time it was successful. Small flames began dancing from the wound in the demon's chest, then they became fiercer and began to consume him. He looked at the faces of his captors, displaying no gratification at their own success in the final moments of their enemy's life. Shania fell to her knees to pray for him …

why would she do that?

The red, amber and golden flames became higher and fiercer. Seconds later, this demon was no more. A small pile of black dust now replaced the once living creature.

Jaz moved forward to collect the chain which appeared untouched, shiny and gold. She picked it up cautiously discovering it to be surprisingly cold, then she kissed it before returning it to Mac.

"Thank you," he said, placing the precious relic inside a pocket of his coat. He then walked over to where Shania and the old man were sitting, on one of the stones. He sat down beside her, took hold of her left hand, which wore his mother's engagement ring and kissed it.

"Are you alright?" he asked, in his well-spoken, privately educated voice.

Shania nodded and smiled. Mac then addressed the others, "Is everyone okay?"

All acknowledged, but Taylor couldn't stop himself from mimicking a comical Sergeant Major's voice, saluting and over-dramatically responding with, "Sir! Yes Sir! All present and correct Sir!"

The old man smiled, the others did too, except for Jaz, who considered him *childish and irritating* sometimes.

The face of the old man suddenly appeared confused as a question had entered his head and required an answer, "I don't understand," he said, in his broad Lincolnshire accent, "Your weapon ... it's ... modern?"

Taylor replied, "The gun has recently been crafted, but the bullets are originally melted-down ancient arrowheads."

Mac continued to explain, "They were discovered in an Egyptian tomb on one of my great, great-grandfather's *digs*. Recent tests made on one of the heads interestingly revealed that it contained minute pieces of asteroid."

Taylor added, "I was able to make four bullets from one single arrowhead. We do not, unfortunately, have a never-ending supply of them."

The old man was once again content, having had the mystery clarified.

The following few moments were quiet and solemn as feelings of relief, excitement and exhaustion began to surface.

Stephen and Gemma were sitting on another stone block, Gemma's aching head resting upon Stephen's broad shoulder. Loudly and carelessly, she suddenly broke the silence, "Okay guys. I've had enough excitement for one night and I need coffee!"

Mac responded, "Great idea!" Then to Shania he whispered, "Are you coming back to mine tonight?"

"I'd better not," she replied, "I really need to get up early tomorrow and begin finalising a flat-mate; I want to spruce-up my spare room a bit and I have a few applications to respond to. But I will pop into the shop tomorrow afternoon if that's alright?"

"Of course," he said, hiding his disappointment. "I had a few interesting antiques come into the shop this week I think you will like." Shania gave him a gentle kiss on his lips.

As everyone rose to their feet, Taylor announced, "I had better call Howard and Zoe and fill them in with everything. I will let them know that the *problem* has been dealt with."

Stephen replied solemnly, "Taylor, I am pretty sure that this *problem* we had tonight is just the beginning."

The elderly man led the small group of weary warriors silently out of the ancient Church, a place so embedded in British history and religion. Each one thanked him as they headed for their vehicles. Thankfully, none of the surrounding properties showed signs of being disturbed.

As Taylor drove his car past the field behind the moonlit ruin, he stopped so that he and his occupants could admire the beautiful horse that had galloped over to greet them. The powerful animal looked spellbindingly beautiful under the illumination of the moonlight. He seemed like he was pleased to see them. Having placed his huge head over the fence to look at them more closely, the mighty stallion then cantered over to a huge tree at the far end of his domain. He stared back, proudly at his leaving admirers.

It had been a long and challenging night. The return journey, through leafy country lanes and the brighter busier roads of Lincoln, were thankfully calm and without drama. A light conversation transpired.

Mac shifted slightly in his front passenger seat, to turn and speak to Shania. "Have you had any possible candidates for a flat-mate yet?" he asked, then continued, "Though why you do not simply sell the place and move in with me, I don't know. You spend more time at mine than yours anyway!"

Taylor and Jaz grinned as they knew what was coming next.

"I like being independent, Mac, you know that!" Shania responded irritably, "Anyway, we are not married yet. And in answer to your question, I have been exchanging emails with a really nice girl in Essex. I think we would get along well together."

Mac appeared concerned, "Make sure you check her out thoroughly first, please."

Shania replied, "Please stop worrying about this. I have done my research; she is **not** on any social media, though I did manage to find a picture of her on-line, performing on stage with the worship band at her church where her dad was the Vicar. The only family she had were her parents who sadly, died from Covid."

"Wow, that sucks," said Taylor.

"Sounds like she is a good candidate to me," Jaz replied coldly,

"You need to pay your bills and we need to keep our circle as small and tight as possible." Everyone agreed.

That night, back in their home, Howard and Zoe breathed sighs of great relief on receiving Taylor's call.

"Everyone is alright," Howard reassured Zoe as soon as Taylor had spoken his first words.

After a brief conversation with Taylor, when plans had been made to meet up the following day, Howard and Zoe finally sat down with their pot of tea and finished off the whole packet of chocolate biscuits.

FRIENDS

The new young vicar, his wife and four small children arrived early, excited to finally be moving into their new home and Parish. Leah had spent the past few months sorting, cleaning and clearing the house, so it was tidy and welcoming for the new tenants. She had her suitcase, backpack and guitar placed in a corner of the entrance hall, all ready to move out once the keys had been handed over.

Following an exchange of kind words, condolences for Leah's loss and wishes for her to have a happy future, Leah wished the family well and walked out of the front door for the very last time, and into the street outside. She stood back, looking up at the only home she could remember and took a moment to say her own private farewell.

Though Pam and William had been overly protective and strict parents, Leah had loved them dearly and her carefree loving spirit had brought love, humour, joy and deep purpose to their lives. She had never envisioned a future without them and had happily accepted their suggestion of attending a local university after completing her exams at school. However, things were different now.

Pam and William had left Leah well provided for in their wills. She had always known that their house came with William's job and she had been given extra time, due to the *Covid lockdowns*, to consider her options. She could have found somewhere close-by to live and study to become a teacher, as she had planned. However, again and again, she thought about the contents of the old biscuit tin.

Here, in Leigh-on-Sea, Leah had her church, the band, her parents' friends and she knew the area well. On the other hand, to her knowledge she had never been outside of Essex, had money of her own nor ever been on an adventure. She was now also aware that *she might even have some blood relatives living in Lincolnshire.* Searching on-line for details of her real mother, Rose, had been of little help in answering her many burning questions.

Leah had made her final decision after exchanging emails with a kind young woman in Lincoln who was searching for a flat mate. This young woman, called Shania, had also been able to advise her on her application to the university there and of the process of qualifying as a Primary School Teacher. Now, although Leah felt scared and a little apprehensive, she also had some hope – and faith that she could make a new happy life for herself in Lincolnshire.

So, having sold her car, Leah took the short walk to the bus-stop, travelled to the bus-station where she caught the coach to London. From London, she got on the train to Lincoln where she found herself delivered to the City Centre. She found the block of flats a short walk away, just as Shania had described.

The block was quite modern, overlooking the Marina with its many interesting boats, elegant swans and the impressive Waterfront, complete with fancy restaurants and a cinema.

Leah took the lift to the fourth floor, as instructed and knocked on the correct door. Shania opened it immediately with a warm and welcoming greeting. Leah and Shania instantly liked one another, and a deep, loyal and life-long friendship was born – both were beautiful in their own unique way. They also shared a childish, silly humour and both appeared, to the world outside as naive sweet innocents, yet were actually strong, extraordinary and intelligent women who had experienced much suffering and loss in their young lives.

Shania had shown Leah to her room; freshly painted in magnolia, all prepared with the bed made-up. There was also a wardrobe, chest of drawers with a mirror, bedside cabinet with a lamp and a desk.

"Right then," Shania announced, "Just park your stuff in here as I'm taking you out for dinner to celebrate your first night in Lincoln."

They took a short walk along a footpath overlooking the water and stopped for a few seconds to appreciate the beautiful surroundings. It was a bright warm day and Shania pointed out a few places of interest and gave directions which led to the different parts of the City. She explained the most interesting, but exhausting way, to go to the Castle and Cathedral Quarter by walking up Steep Hill, with its individual and interesting little shops. She explained where the doctor, dentist and certain stores were situated – including her fiancé's antique shop. Then she described the narrow stone steps at the side of the old Tudor building, that were easily missed yet so convenient.

Enjoying their delicious vegan meal, Shania had asked Leah about her past life as the daughter of a Vicar.

"My parents were both very religious," Leah said, "My dad took his calling seriously. I am afraid I must have been a little of a disappointment to him, when I reflect on my youthful behaviour."

"Oh, do tell! Come on, spill the beans!" Shania urged.

Leah bit her bottom lip then began, "Well, I would get the giggles at the worst possible times – especially when a particular parishioner called Edith, sang in her operatic voice. Even if it was at a funeral! I used to pretend that I had dropped something on the floor, just to give myself a chance to compose myself, but when I looked back up again, I would see my dad staring down at me, giving me ... *the look*. And I was always questioning their beliefs, finding bits of it funny, other bits disturbing and some of it, well ... and ..."

Shania had pretended to fall asleep, then in a dry voice, she teased, "Wow! I need to warn my friends about you, don't I? You're clearly a real *wild one*."

Eyes met and hysterical fits of laughter ensued.

In the weeks that followed, Leah filled her time whilst waiting to begin her studies, singing, playing her guitar and composing new songs in her room. Shania was often absent due to *work commitments and staying at her boyfriend, Mac's,* but she enjoyed listening to Leah's songs whenever she made it home to their flat. Sometimes they would go out for some dinner or breakfast together, everything had been going so well, until ...

One night, Shania came home late and was surprised to find the flat completely quiet and dark. Flicking the light-switch on, she was momentarily shocked discovering that a blackbird had flown in through an open window and must have got trapped inside.

The poor creature became highly stressed, flapping its wings and darting from one end of the room to the other, screeching the whole time. Shania managed to catch it, then release it through the window.

It had been an extremely unpleasant and noisy experience, so Shania assumed Leah could not have been home or she would surely have heard the commotion – certainly, the sound from the ornaments, falling off the shelf! However, the sudden sounds coming from Leah's bedroom alerted her that it was not the case. Slowly opening the door and switching on the light, she found Leah in a pool of sweat. She was moaning, murmuring things ... names ... places ... something about a *flame,* but was not conscious.

Having immediately called Mac, Shania put a cold wet folded

flannel on Leah's burning brow. Her hair was sticking to her face in tight damp curls as Shania wiped them away from her eyes.

"Leah, Leah, what has happened?" she whispered gently. Her friend's breathing became less erratic, "Everything is alright. You must not be frightened, all will be fine."

Leah was slowly gaining consciousness, she could see and feel Shania wiping her face with the flannel, but she could also hear a man's well-spoken voice coming from the other room.

"Yes, that is exactly what she was saying. But she seems to be coming around now so I will leave and let Shania take care of her." The conversation then finished with him saying, "Will you cancel *Doc,* or do you want me to call him? ... Okay, thank you ... Yes. No problem. Bye Howard."

Shania spent the rest of the night, watching over her friend and was astounded the following morning when Leah awoke, having not remembered any of the disturbing events from the previous night and was feeling merely *tired, with a bit of a heavy head.*

That same evening, Shania brought Mac back to the flat to introduce him to Leah. Leah immediately felt like she had already heard his voice before and was pleased to finally meet her best friend's fiancé. She was pleasantly impressed with the exceptional manners and friendliness of the stylish, handsome and muscular young man. She considered them to be one of those *perfect couples* and Leah and Mac immediately became good friends too. From then onwards, he would drop Shania home most nights and come up to their flat for a coffee and chat with them both. He was gregarious and spoke passionately of his love for his work in the antique trade and of the interesting items he had recently acquired.

In a short time, Leah had made a new life for herself and she was happy for the first time in a very long while. She had a nice home in a beautiful city; she had her music, her studies and most of all, she had made two life-long friends.

TIME TRAVELLERS

Zachariah, The Child –

Tiberias Galilee, 20 Ce

T he young boy of six years old, with dark eyes, tanned skin and black curly hair sat patiently on his young mother's lap. She was using a cloth and a small bowl of precious water to wash away the day's dust and grime from her son's face. Zachariah loved the feeling of the cool refreshing cloth against his burning cheeks. On completing bathing his face, neck and hands, Martha smiled before pinching his nose, causing them both to giggle.

At that moment, Zachariah's father, Ananias, entered their small home of mortar-and-stone walls, partly cut into the limestone hillside.

He observed the scene before him then asked, "Why is the boy not yet asleep in his bed? He has worked hard this day."

Zachariah felt pleased and proud to hear these words of praise coming from his elderly and revered father. For Ananias already had eight grown-up sons from his previous wife, Salome. When Salome had died, Ananias' close friend had persuaded him during his grief, to take his own eldest daughter, Martha's, hand in marriage. This would provide Ananias with companionship and care throughout his old age and for Martha, a husband known to be a kind well respected member of their community. Though cynical of taking such a young bride at his time of life, Ananias had agreed and to his joy, found her to be a good wife. With intelligent conversation, she was extremely pleasing to behold, hard-working and she gave him another son within their first year of marriage.

Having raised other children, Ananias was experienced and aware that his youngest son was intelligent like his mother and braver than any child he had ever known. He loved Zachariah with all his heart, but he also looked forward to spending the evenings alone with his sweet wife.

"I am going to sleep now, Papa." Zachariah announced. Martha lifted him off her lap and walked with him to the far end of their home, where a space had been cut into the rock creating a small place for a bed. Although it lay upon the hard mud floor, it was comfortable; made with straw and a soft blanket. A curtain, a metre high, provided privacy.

As he lay drifting in and out of sleep, Zachariah could hear the flies as he wiped sweat from his face. It was another hot evening and he was extremely tired. However, he had not been sleeping well recently having overheard conversations between the other men of the village, while he worked, lifting and removing heavy rocks from the fields for farming.

They spoke fearfully of the rumours of a group of rogue soldiers, under the command of General Raama who were in the area burning villages and leaving no survivors. They spoke of a *flame* that must not be allowed to get into the hands of the 'evil ones' at all costs. The fear in the voices of the men had worried Zachariah. Now he was thinking about it again and sleep was becoming impossible.

Suddenly, he heard someone knocking on their door.

Ananias opened it as Martha's father burst inside. "The *flame* has been taken by our best rider, out of the village to safety this very night! Our scouts have informed us Raama's army is heading our way!"

Next, Zachariah heard his mother's voice, "Fear not my Father, nor my Husband. Our Lord will protect us."

Then came the sound of distant riders, getting closer.

"I must go to my wife," his grandfather said, "Pray our God is with us this night!"

Seconds later, the gates of Hell were flung wide open as chaos and carnage ensued. Zachariah froze in his bed, listening to the screams from the dying outside. He could hear the sounds of horses, chomping on their bits, crushing men beneath their gigantic hooves and the shouting voices of the relentless unforgiving soldiers.

The door burst open and two soldiers entered. One wickedly smiled on seeing Martha. Zachariah could see only the feet of those inside his home. He watched his father run forward and the sound of a sword slicing through his flesh. Moaning, Ananias fell to the floor and was no more.

Just as Zachariah was about to run from his hiding place behind the curtain, to avenge his father, his mother took one of the knives she used for cutting meat from the table and thrust it into her own body. The soldiers laughed as she fell to the ground with her face close to the curtain.

In her dying breath, Martha whispered to her precious son, "Be still."

As the cruel amused soldiers left, Zachariah could contain his fury no more. Grabbing hold of another knife from the table, he charged out of the door and rammed it into the thigh of the nearest soldier he could find.

Suddenly, the chaos ceased as all the soldiers stopped to watch the reaction of their menacing leader.

Raama, paused, withdrew the blade from deep within his thigh without a flinch nor murmur and turned around to see the small enraged child stood before him. A soldier stepped forward, lifting his sword intending to strike the boy down. However, Raama grabbed hold of the long blade before it reached the child's head. With his hand miraculously intact and unbelievably uninjured, Raama swiped the soldier's head sending him flying through the air and landing on the ground with his face covered in blood.

"What is your name, boy?" Raama asked.

Raama stared into the young black pools of hatred that were staring defiantly right back at him. "Well, are you going to beg me to spare your life, or not?"

"Never!" came the infant's bold reply.

"I suppose you are praying to your God thinking He will help you?" Raama scathed, then laughed. The soldiers laughed.

Raama was then intrigued, fascinated, at the young child's bold answer, "My parents named me Zachariah. Their God has betrayed my family," he said, "He has betrayed me and I will never forgive Him. But I will kill you, whether it be in this life or the next, for I will call upon everything that is evil from the depths of Sheol to help me!"

Raama was stunned; never had he come across such bravery or defiance in a mortal man – a boy! Seconds later, the soldiers rode away from the burning village leaving blood covered bodies scattered everywhere.

Raama had slapped the child rendering him unconscious, thrown him upon a horse and rode away with his *own personal experiment*. Zachariah's life had been spared that night, but he was to awake the following morning to a despicable and miserable future.

14 Years Later – The Soldier

The raging battle between the two weary sides had been fer-
ociously fought. Tobias, with his group of men and women,
bravely and heroically defended their village in a territory
where Raama and his legion were obliterating every settlement
in sight.

Stars twinkled down from the black velvet night sky, onto the
atrocity beneath. Burning torches and small fires suppressed
the stench of the dead. Murmurs and cries from the wounded
were rife. Only a handful of Tobias' people had been spared;
those considered *useful* to Raama's army. Exhausted, trembling
with fear, they had been herded to the centre of the makeshift
camp.

Raama had been resting on a large rock, staring into the flames
of his small burning fire when he noticed Zachariah walking
his way. Now a tall, strong and handsome young man, he was
fearless and obedient as Tribunus Laticlavius, Raama's right
hand man. Raama watched Zachariah become distracted by the
screams of a young prisoner, being forced to leave the group by
two revolting soldiers. One managed to drag her, kicking and
fighting for her life, in the direction of a large tree, after the
other coward had spinelessly and forcefully slapped her almost
unconscious. Their pathetic laughter soon ceased when they
were confronted by Zachariah.

"What do you think you are doing?" he asked them, cold and
expressionless.

"Just having a little fun?" one of the cowardly buffoons replied
sheepishly.

"You will not call it 'fun' when she puts poison in your food, you *fool*. Return her to the others and treat her well, or I will deal with you – do you understand?"

The calm tone yet authoritative warning of Zachariah's command, terrorised them with fear. Almost falling over themselves to perform their orders, the weeping young girl was returned to the group of captives who were watching events closely.

On her return, a young man – the girl's brother – called out to Zachariah, "Thank you for showing her mercy. You are a good man."

Zachariah stood still, turned around slowly and coldly replied, "There is no such thing as *mercy*. And no, I am not."

On reaching the warmth of the flames, Zachariah took out his leather flask of water and thirstily drank, swallowing large gulps.

Raama had been watching him closely, "Something is wrong with you, what is it?" he said.

"I am cut, just a little; I will be fine," Zachariah replied, attempting to wrap his red woollen cape tightly around himself. However, he could not conceal the flowing blood rapidly soaking through the fabric of his tunic, dripping off the strips of steel that should have protected his broad muscular chest. The water had not cured his parched mouth and dry cracked lips, he suddenly felt cold and weak.

Sitting down beside Raama, Zachariah had little peace as Raama began waving his arms around, "Why? Tell me why do you constantly put yourself in harm's way for these *fools*? I watched you in the battle today, yet again, defending the backs of him … and him … and him! You are important to me! *They* are not! Why do you always do it?"

There was nothing Zachariah could do to prevent the full weight of his body from slowly slumping painfully and uncontrollably, to the ground.

Soldiers began crowding around, not out of concern for Zachariah, rather to watch the reaction of their formidable Ruler witness *his favourite, his prodigy*, lay dying.

Raama, for the first time in his existence, was displaying signs of concern ... compassion ... traits unseen before! He knelt down beside Zachariah, shielding his still body, then shouted at the twisted audience, "Get away! The lot of you!"

With this, all dispersed, with a few murmurings of, "Yes Legatus."

Zachariah was now beginning to lose consciousness; he knew he was dying, and it felt good. His life since having his family and childhood ripped away from him had been a reality of violent survival and nothing more than a painful lonely existence. He could hear his mother's sweet voice calling to him. For the first time in many years, he allowed himself to remember her face, her beauty, tenderness and love.

For a second, he thought he could feel her gentle kiss upon his cheek then her soothing voice whispering to him, "Be still. Be still."

He could again remember the feeling of joy, of love ... and ...

PAIN! SO MUCH PAIN!

Striking intrusively through his mother's soothing tones came a louder, powerful and sadistic vocal sound. Replacing his tender mother's touch, instead came violent shaking and hard slaps across his face.

"Listen to me, damn you! Wake up! Wake up!" Raama demanded.

Zachariah did not want to wake up! He would have chosen to have died on that night however it was not to be, and he would spend the following two millenniums regretting it.

As excruciating pain shot throughout every vein, his bones felt like they were breaking all at once. A burning fire had ignited in his abdomen, exploding, hurling and scolding throughout his entire body.

"No! ... Please! ... No!" Zachariah begged Raama, grabbing hold of his arm. But Raama was kneeling over him; chanting, reciting verses in an *unnatural* and unrecognisable language of this world.

Suddenly, Zachariah's body convulsed uncontrollably, his fingers digging deeply into the hard, dry ground. Then ... silence.

Following this came an instant relief from his physical pain.

Next ... consciousness ... extreme awareness ... intense observance and hearing ... tremendous strength with agility ... and perfect perception.

For Raama had decided, in his arrogance and egotism, that he wanted Zachariah to serve him and the master to whom *he* served, throughout eternity.

Those souls present on that evening, would someday die, as all mortals do, but Raama – one of *Evil's own* and his servant, Zachariah – created and born from mortal flesh, would walk through the ages of time, with the future generations of this world.

France – Early September 1307 Ad

Having each received orders and instructions from King Philip IV, the troupe of men had assembled in the large hall, many having travelled countless treacherous miles across land and sea. Their clandestine orders were to report to the large hall of this remote Monastery, home to a unit of Benedictine Monks, reliably more dedicated to the service of their *Earthly King*, than their *Heavenly one.*

Whispered, confused and nervous voices echoed around the cold high stone, walls. All hushed as the King entered the hall and sat on a large chair placed for him at the front. His entourage of courtiers remained in the corner, however a large intimidating man with a black beard and of affluent appearance, stood on his right-hand side. For Raama was now an advisor to Philip, having a macabre hold over his thoughts and actions. He was feared by those in the royal household, above the king himself.

The following few minutes were to send a spine-chilling fear into the hearts and souls of all those present. For Philip announced that all who had been summoned, *his secret eyes and ears from around the world*, were to be the elite couriers of his Royal Orders.

Philip, under the direction of Raama had devised a plan to systematically eradicate the wealthy, influential defenders and guardians of the Christian Church – The Knights Templars. The well-organised plot was to begin on Friday, 13th October, all across Europe and beyond.

The couriers were each given their documents and dispatched out into the night.

Zachariah had been stood at the back of the hall, watching for signs of defiance or unrest upon hearing the instructions. He had spotted none. However, he had noticed uninvited eyes, peering through a small peephole from behind a stone wall. His investigations led him to a secret underground passage, leading from a small trapdoor outside, hidden among a small randomly planted group of bushes.

Creeping silently through the dark tunnel, Zachariah reached some wooden steps which led up to a small secret cavity within the inner wall of the hall. On reaching the top of the steps, he was greeted by an elderly monk. Caught by surprise, the monk was clearly terrified by his discoverer.

"What are you doing?" Zachariah asked coldly.

"Nothing!" came the feeble reply. "I ... I often come here for private prayer, the place has been so busy and noisy today ... I ... I have overheard nothing."

Zachariah stared into the old man's weary and worn out face then said, "You have heard too much."

"Please?" the monk begged, "If the strongest opposition to *Evil* are destroyed, they are the only protectors of peace – the wicked will have no opposition. Think, young man, just consider the consequences of that!"

Zachariah stood still, staring for a moment into timeworn troubled eyes. Then suddenly, from inside a pocket of his thick woollen robe, the monk withdrew a knife and thrusted it into Zachariah's chest.

"I am sorry," he mumbled, "but I must warn the Pope!"

Expecting Zachariah to collapse to the floor, the old man began to limp towards the steps. However, looking back round at Zachariah, he was petrified to see he had withdrawn the knife from his muscular body and was still stood tall, completely unscathed.

"Your Pope already knows," Zachariah said, "He is as greedy and as jealous of the Knights as your very own precious Abbot and King are."

The old man could not comprehend what had just happened, nor what had been revealed.

"No!" he cried, "No! What kind of evil magic is this? You are a deceiver!"

Zachariah walked slowly towards the monk, holding the knife. Believing his death was imminent, the monk closed his eyes and began to pray. However, to his surprise, Zachariah presented him with his own knife, with its handle facing forward.

"Go ... just go ... accept what is to be," Zachariah said, "Live out the rest of your life peacefully. There is nothing you can do about this, old man."

Thomas, this old monk who now had a limp and coughed throughout the winter months, had once been a fearless young knight who had fought in Crusades and defended the defenceless. He had believed in good, fought and won many battles, loved a beautiful woman and raised a son. His war-wounds and the death of his wife were reasons enough for him to retire and retreat to a spiritual existence within the Church.

Questioning a soul he did not, or could not understand, staring into the dark eyes of anger and pain, Thomas replied, "I will accept the future if you can. Your words are truthful when you say that there is nothing I alone can do about it."

With this, Zachariah took a step backwards, allowing him to pass.

Zachariah had unknowingly, allowed Thomas to leave the monastery forever that night. To travel many miles, concealing a small jewelled box made of gold, containing a small eternal *flame*. It was a *miraculous* treasure, entrusted to him as a young knight. It had become his duty, his quest to make the long dangerous trek and pass on this religious relic to his son. For Zachariah had revealed the shocking truth to him; those at the monastery could not be trusted to protect it.

Thomas was blessed to spend the remaining months of his life enjoying the peace and love at the home of his son, daughter-in-law and their three young children, on their large wealthy estate in the rural East Midlands of England.

September 1620 Boston, Lincolnshire England

One hundred and thirty men, women and children, along with sheep, goats, chickens and dogs had been herded onboard the mighty vessel. The Pilgrims from Boston, Lincolnshire had been transferred to The Mayflower which had set sail from Plymouth. It was sailing across the wide Atlantic Ocean taking the persecuted to a new and exciting life, their escape to religious freedom in The New World.

The overcrowded ship with its high sides made sailing difficult, the journey would take twice as long as it could have, a gruelling 66 days.

Onboard were Paul, his wife Margaret and daughter, Alice. Alice had inherited the most unusual bright green eyes from her father and was a pretty sweet natured girl of fifteen.

Also, on board was Paul's life-long friend, Joseph with his wife Rebecca and son, David. Their small group had decided to stay together and were a supportive extended family unit. There were very few places where anyone could be alone, but Alice and David somehow managed to seek a time and place where they could share precious tender moments together each day.

One evening, with just a few days remaining of their long voyage, the group shared their usual meal consisting of dried meat, fruit and stale biscuits. The youths were quieter than usual.

"What is the matter with you, boy, you've not eaten your biscuit?" enquired Joseph. "If you are not going to eat it, I will – as disgusting as it is!"

The others laughed. The fresh-faced lad got up from the floor and walked round to Alice, who stood up quickly and held his hand. They both looked terrified as David began to speak.

"I beg your pardon, Father, Mother, Paul and Margaret, but we have something we wish to ask you."

David bit his lip and took a deep breath as he could feel Alice tightly squeezing his hand, giving him the courage he needed to address their captive and curious audience.

"Well," he began, "there is no other way of saying this ... but ... well ..."

Interrupting him, Alice blurted out impatiently, "We love each other, we want to get married. Please Papa? Please do not be cross!"

With the wind suddenly taken from his sails, David looked nervously around at the others.

"Yes," he added, "like she said, we want to be together, always."

Immediately, both Paul and Benjamin jumped up and hugged one another.

"See! I told you he would!" Benjamin laughed while dancing with joy. Margaret and Rebecca stood and hugged the bewildered-faced young couple.

"Oh, this is a happy evening indeed!" cried Margaret.

The following day, all onboard were invited to share in the joys of a wedding at sea. Alice wore silk flowers in her hair, a precious gift from her mother-in-law, to be. Holding a bunch of dried herbs tied with a ribbon and wearing the best of her three only dresses, Alice made a beautiful bride. Her handsome and older husband to be, of almost seventeen years, was a dashing groom, wearing his father's one and only smart jacket.

The priest of choice, for there were many religious leaders on board, joined the two sweethearts together, in life and death, witnessed by all the passengers, including the two *mysterious passengers* who were the talk of them all.

The *two men* who had made little conversation with any of the other passengers since departing the dock had spent the long tedious hours onboard, above, on the frantic deck, isolating themselves away from everyone else. However, no matter how *invisible* Raama and Zachariah had tried to be, they had certainly been noticed. For the men were both extremely handsome, oozed wealth and importance and neither wore a wedding ring.

After the short but sweet wedding vows had been promised, a little singing and dancing began to take place. Zachariah noticed Raama go and speak to David. He appeared to be congratulating him though Zachariah then saw his short whisper into David's ear and the look of fury suddenly appear upon the young man's face.

Unnoticed by everyone else excepting Zachariah and David, Raama then casually walked over to where Alice was busy behind a curtain, preparing a bed for her new husband and self, in the gap that had been made between the two families' spaces.

A moment later, Alice appeared from behind the curtain shaken, tears in her eyes and a rip in her dress from the shoulder all the way across the bodice to her waist. Still unnoticed, David furiously followed Raama up onto the deck. Quickly grabbing and wrapping her shawl around herself, for Alice feared the worst for her new precious husband, she ran after them both, unobserved by anyone else but Zachariah.

Seconds later, Zachariah saw Raama had reappeared and was speaking with an excitable and blushing mother and her equally flirtatious daughter.

After a while, the newly wedded couple were missed, and a

search began. It only took a couple of minutes on deck before a loud scream alerted everyone to the sight of the crewmember covered in blood, holding a knife and standing over the butchered bodies of the two young lovers.

A crazed mob beat the dazed crewmember to death in seconds, although he continued shouting his innocence till the end.

The following day, Zachariah stood on deck, beside Raama, at the sea burial service for the two cherished teenagers, unlike the secret and crude burial of which the innocent spellbound sailor's body had received.

"So ... why? What was the purpose?" Zachariah asked icily of his master.

Raama shrugged arrogantly, "It had to be done. We could not risk those two bloodlines uniting. It could have caused us a lot of trouble in the future. It is lucky we were here to stop it. The *one we both serve* is in our debt."

Zachariah was quiet and thoughtful. He was watching the grieving parents when he noticed Margaret rub the swelling in her abdomen.

"Come," he said quickly to Raama, "Let us leave the grieving to their grief."

Zachariah was not to know that he had witnessed Margaret touching the son who was growing inside of her, a child with striking green eyes who would grow up and someday marry the daughter of Benjamin and Rebecca, born two years after arriving in Massachusetts. For someday, their descendants would be spread across the whole world and were to be the *thorns* in Raama's side.

CHRISTMASTIME

Lincoln - The Present

With just two weeks remaining until Christmas, Leah had sent her virtual Christmas wishes to a few people back in Leigh-on-Sea, Essex and personally given her hand-written cards to her new university friends in Lincoln. The only two cards she had held on to were Shania's and Mac's. She had bought them both presents; expensive perfume and after-shave and intended to give the cards and presents together, to her dearest friends on Christmas morning.

Shania had insisted that Leah agree to spend Christmas with her and Mac at his house. A couple of days spent with her friends, a promise of watching old movies, indulging in chocolates, mince-pies and mulled wine were an offer she found difficult to refuse. She could not admit to feeling excited about Christmas, missing her parents so deeply, however, it was certainly going to help make the season feel a lot nicer than she had ever thought possible.

This evening, Mac had brought Shania home a little earlier than usual. Considering how cold it was outside, they both appeared to be sweating and Shania immediately had a shower before returning to their lounge where Leah had made them all coffee.

"So," Shania began, having sat herself comfortably next to Mac on the small fabric sofa and directly opposite Leah. "Christmas Eve, there is a social event being held at our ... church. We would like you to come with us and then we can all go back to Mac's to enjoy the rest of Christmas. What do you say?"

Leah was slightly surprised by this as Shania had never once mentioned that she and Mac belonged to a church. Knowing Leah's background, Leah thought it very odd that this had never came up in discussion before.

"You never told me that you attend church?" she quizzed them, "Which one?"

Mac replied, "Have you ever heard anyone at your university mention in conversation, *The Forum*?"

"Yes," said Leah, "But it was in the context of sport activities, educational and fun courses ... that sort of thing."

"Well," Shania began, "The Forum is a different place to different people. It is a church, though it praises the good things in our lives rather than practising any one particular religion and it serves the community with many charitable causes. It is a sports centre; it is also a place of learning offering lots of courses. People can access free advice, counselling and support, either face-to-face or virtually. I work there myself twice a week."

Shania paused for breath, then having checked for Leah's sustained interest, proudly continued.

"The building can safely accommodate a large congregation; it has the best technology with security equipment and devices that purify the air and check the temperature and basic physical wellness of every person that enters. Our virtual members are from all around the world, having never once stepped inside the building. We have a good pastor and a great worship band with thousands of online followers."

Leah knew that Shania was a professional counsellor and had considered herself most fortunate having been on the receiving end of her friend's expert advice over the past few months.

Leah asked jokingly, "Have you been there tonight, working out or something? It must have been a tough session as you're still both sweating!"

Suddenly, Leah was aware of a new mood and atmosphere within the room. Her friends looked awkward and uncomfortable.

Shania responded quickly, "Yes, we have a friend called Jaz who teaches various Self-Defence and Martial Arts classes there. Mac and I enjoy attending them, don't we?" Mac nodded thoughtfully.

"Okay," Leah announced, "I would love to come to this ... social. It will be a new experience for me and something special to look forward to. Last Christmas was ... awful, and the past Christmas parties at my parents' church were always interesting! I remember we had the same DJ every year, Mr Ivor Good, fondly known in church as *I've a good C.D. player*! He played the same old stuff year in and year out. And my mum always made these cute little angel cup-cakes, that even the grown-ups looked forward to."

Then following a moment of reflection, she added, "It's strange when I look back now, how I used to moan and whinge to my parents about going, yet I enjoyed every single one of those parties." Adding thoughtfully, "I felt happy ... and safe, back then."

"Why would you **not** ever feel safe, Leah?" asked Shania softly.

"I ... don't know," came Leah's profound response.

Christmas Eve

It was almost seven-thirty. The roads and pavements glistened on this icy-cold evening and Leah was feeling a little anxious, waiting outside the apartment block for Shania and Mac to collect her. Her smart new travel bag bought especially for the occasion, was packed with carefully chosen clothes, toiletries and Christmas gifts and goodies, and placed on the frosty ground beside her.

Tonight, would be the first social occasion Leah had been invited to and accepted since before the death of her parents.

Suddenly, she recognised Mac's black sporty Jaguar pull up beside her. Mac emerged from the driving seat and collected her bag, carefully placing it in the boot. Shania jumped out from the passenger's side and eased her seat forward, allowing Leah to climb inside.

"Happy Christmas Eve!" Shania exclaimed excitedly once Leah was sat comfortably at the back.

"Everything okay?" Mac checked before gently pulling away into the busy traffic.

"Oh, definitely, thank you," Leah replied. For she was now feeling much better; relieved that she had chosen and decided on the appropriate outfit for the evening. Like herself, she had noticed that Mac and Shania were wearing smart black jeans. She thoughtfully thanked herself for not picking her restrictive long red and black chiffon dress, with uncomfortable high black court shoes that were now thrown and disregarded, across her bedroom floor. Instead, she had settled on her feminine violet sparkly blouse, her jeans, smart casual jacket and black boots. Shania had also selected a pretty blouse and Mac wore a white silk shirt, opened at the neck and his sleeves casually rolled up to his elbows.

Inside the car, Leah felt cosy and comfortable in the luxurious leather seat. She could smell the combination of leather, sweet perfume and masculine cologne and she appreciated the beautiful calming orchestral music that was coming from ... somewhere discreet. She was in no hurry to reach their destination. However, it did not take long, driving out of the City Centre and shortly arriving at The Forum.

The well-lit carpark looked busy, so Mac was pleased to find a parking space close to the building. Leah surveyed the incredible structure as she climbed out from the back seat, while Shania held the door open.

"Wow!" she said, "It's big ... and very impressive."

Leah began to put on her new black glittery face mask.

Shania smiled, "It is, isn't it?" Then added, "You won't be needing that."

As Mac began to escort Shania and Leah to the steps leading up to the entrance, Stephen and Gemma arrived on their motorcycles.

Mac did the introductions, "Leah, we would like you to meet Stephen, a Lecturer of Religious Studies at the university, and his wife Gemma, a Professor of Languages. Guys, this is Leah."

"I'm so pleased to meet you both!" Leah smiled.

Stephen returned her pleasant greeting however Gemma appeared cool and distant, avoiding eye contact and was unsociable, choosing not to join in the friendly chatter that ensued as they all entered The Forum together.

Once inside, Leah immediately noticed the beautiful Christmas tree and exquisite decorations. The band, playing in the Main Hall could be heard through the quality sound system installed throughout the entire building.

Stephen and Gemma went directly upstairs, leaving the others to venture further inside. Leah noticed a large festive table by the kitchen area, displaying brown paper lunch bags, tied with shiny coloured ribbons and bows. There were also recyclable cups and cans of pop.

Shania noticed Leah's interest and explained, "That is the party food for everyone. We all get a bag of delicious goodies later."

"I'm looking forward to it!" Leah replied honestly. She could see two men and a woman, wearing hygiene gloves and masks, filling more bags with scrumptious delights. The tempting smell from the small tubs of curried vegetables, carefully placed into each bag, were making her feel hungry.

Shania found them a table, close to the entrance of the Main Hall. Leah could see through the large open doors to the band performing on the professional stage, complete with the best lighting and sound system that money could buy. The drummer played inside his own opaque booth, while two keyboard players, a base guitarist, two rhythm guitarists, four vocalists and a lead vocalist, also playing lead guitar, entertained.

Shania noticed Leah's interest in the technician and his filming equipment. She explained, "Most events held in the Main Hall are recorded for those wishing to be part of the church services and other functions, from the comfort and safety of their own homes. Courses and lectures held in the classrooms upstairs are also recorded."

Leah was finding the whole experience enlightening and inspiring. Just a few months ago, she had been convinced that the whole world had been turned upside down, with many of its inhabitants landing on their brains and going completely crazy; the news correspondents on her television were constantly ridiculing and causing opposition for those in the public eye who were brave enough to step forward and attempt to make the best decisions they could, though often unpopular. So many decent individuals, had quietly and tirelessly, got on with their work and family-life, while becoming increasingly confused by world events. People were turning on each other and the entire world was consumed with accusations and hatred. It had appeared to her that some people cared more about the cancellation of their holiday in a foreign land, than they did about people dying and of the struggling farmers and businesses who supplied the food on their tables.

Now, suddenly, Leah felt like she had some hope again, faith in people once more and optimism in the world's future. After all, the world had recently received a serious wake-up call; a reminder of how precious life, nature and loved-ones are to us all.

Leah smiled and thought of her mother, Pam and how pleased she would have been to know that her daughter had found a place like The Forum. She would have used *her words* to describe it, *a little piece of Heaven, here on Earth.*

Leah now focused on listening to the great songs and watching the performers. The musicians were incredible, the vocal harmonies were without fault and the lead singer, Lenny, was undeniably talented.

Suddenly, the band had finished their set for the first half of the evening and were leaving the stage while a group of teenagers began preparing it for the next piece of entertainment.

Leah turned to see an extremely handsome young man with the most striking green eyes, standing before her, "Hi!" he said, "I'm Taylor. You must be Leah. I have heard a lot about you."

Shania and Mac were busy in conversation with one of the guitarists who had just come off stage. A group of young Street Dancers, dressed in colourful costumes, were now performing to backing tracks.

"Hello, yes I am," she replied shyly.

Taylor continued, "Shania mentioned in conversation that you are a musician and a brilliant singer."

Leah felt herself blush. This was not unnoticed by Taylor, who found it complementary and he was pleased.

"Well, I do enjoy music," Leah said, "Do you play an instrument yourself, Taylor?"

Taylor smiled, revealing perfect white teeth, further increasing his good looks and appeal. Leah swallowed a large gulp of air. Taylor smiled even more and combed his hair through his long masculine fingers.

"I enjoy my work in electronics. I designed and produced all the security and safety innovations for this place. That's *my thing*," he said, proudly.

Now Shania and Mac were free to join their conversation.

"I see you've introduced yourself to Leah, Taylor?" said Shania, with her eyebrows raised.

"Of course, he has." Mac laughed. Leah felt embarrassed yet surprisingly happy as Taylor found a stray chair and placed himself next to her.

Later, in twos, they went and collected their meals and drinks. Leah and Taylor chatted merrily together. On returning to their seats, Leah was approached by the lead singer and guitarist of the band, Lenny.

Lenny, had thin, fluffy ginger hair and a billy-goat beard. He was tall and lanky with pale freckly skin and bright blue eyes.

"Hi," he said, "A little bird has told me that you would make a good member of the band. Would you like to come along and audition in the New Year?"

Leah could have jumped for joy!

"Yes please!" she answered immediately.

Lenny laughed, "Okay," he said, "Rehearsals begin the first Tuesday night of the New Year, at seven. Bring any *dots* with you that you would like to audition with. Prepare two songs. Do not be late!"

"Thank you, thank you so much! And, no, I won't be late!" Leah responded in utter joy, as Lenny walked back inside the Main Hall, returning to his wife and young children seated close to the front of the stage.

"Well, that is exciting, isn't it?" wailed Shania.

"I can't believe it!" Leah cried, "Tonight is like a wonderful dream that I don't want to wake up from!" She noticed the others' strange reaction to her words, though they did all eventually smile at her again. (The last thing they wanted to happen, right now, was for her to experience another one of her *dreams!*)

Towards the end of the evening, Leah, along with her friends, helped the many others who had begun clearing up. Leah noticed a young attractive oriental-looking woman, Jaz, with shocking green hair and noticeable green eyes, talking with Shania. The conversation appeared to be serious and Shania looked worried.

On noticing Leah watching them, Jaz ended the sombre discussion. The two said their farewells, then Shania had an afterthought, "Is Rob off tomorrow?"

"Yes!" Jaz beamed, her face suddenly lighting up, "We will both be there. Neither of us could believe our luck when Rob was actually asked to swap shifts!"

"Ah, that is super!" Shania exclaimed and they exchanged a few quieter last words before parting.

It suddenly occurred to Leah that others had been invited to Mac's Christmas Day soiree, too. Her thoughts then quickly turned to Taylor and she hoped she might be seeing him again very soon.

Later, on the drive back to Mac's house, Shania addressed Leah,

"So, I think you had a good time tonight, eh? I also think a certain young fellow by the name of Taylor, did too!"

"I did! And I hope so!" Leah laughed.

Just a few minutes later, Mac had circled the magnificent and glistening walls of the mighty Cathedral and had driven sharply into a small road and then swung into another tight turning where an electronically controlled gate automatically opened onto a wide driveway. The front garden with extra parking was well hidden by the wall of thick high hedges.

The old but beautifully restored house before her, took Leah's breath away. It was exquisitely charming with original window frames, a large handsome wooden front door and had been tastefully decorated with tiny twinkling stars of light. A sparkling Christmas tree was visible through one of the windows. Leah was now quite sure that Mac was extremely rich, considering his magnificent residence!

If Leah had been impressed by the outside of Mac's abode, then on seeing the inside, left her speechless.

"Wow!" she finally said, breathlessly. "Wow, I have never seen such a beautiful home in all my life."

The inside of the historic and ancient house was unpredictably modern and stylish. It was bright, with white walls and lush furnishings.

The downstairs was open plan with a large extension leading out into a long well-established garden. In the main living area were four large white leather sofas, though other interesting antique chairs were placed strategically around the substantial room. Interesting features such as beautifully coloured patterned rugs, exquisite tapestries and interesting ornaments and curios enhanced and enriched the marvellous yet homely space. A modest sized Christmas Tree stood proudly in the space in front of the wooden framed, leaded windows. It twinkled and sparkled, decorated with colourful lights and a few simple, small and unique trimmings.

The kitchen and dining area spread into the large modern extension. The white hi-spec kitchen had top of the range appliances with marble preparation surfaces, all of which were fitted along one side of the annex, leaving abundant space for eating and entertaining.

The dining area, consisted of a long narrow wooden table with ten leather upholstered chairs, though it could comfortably seat at least twice that number. Ten guest places had been set with white porcelain plates, silver cutlery, crystal water and wine glasses and red napkins. The imaginative and sparkly decorations incorporating natural winter foliage, together with the opulent silver candelabra and red candles created the festive and creative table displays. The floor was attractively tiled throughout, and the space felt larger by having the great walls of glass, cleverly leading the eye to encompass the outside space.

A splendid long garden with a patio and perfect lawn, was bordered by lush plants, tall trees and hedging. Ingenious strategic lighting created a soothing mystical panorama, designed to be especially appreciated in the dark winter evenings.

"I am making coffee, *ladies!*" called Mac, as Shania led Leah through to the kitchen area and pulled out two chrome and white leather stools from below one of the preparation surfaces, creating a convenient breakfast bar.

Mac placed the white mugs down in front of Shania and Leah and drank his own coffee, whilst leaning against a tall American fridge-freezer.

"Looking forward to tomorrow, Leah?" he asked.

"Oh yes, I am. I can see you are having a few other guests for dinner?"

"Yes," he replied, "Our pastor, Howard, and his wife Zoe will be coming. Also, Stephen, Gemma and Taylor, who you have already met."

Leah's heart skipped a beat; she would see Taylor again in just a few short hours!

"Also, our friend Jaz and ..." Mac hesitated and looked inquiringly at Shania, who interrupted him ...

"Yes, Jaz and her partner Rob, will be coming," she confirmed, "I spoke to her earlier and she told me that Rob is not working Christmas Day after all, but I suppose, will be starting an early shift on Boxing Day."

"That's good," Mac replied, "She is always much *nicer* when Rob is around." Shania laughed, but agreed wholeheartedly.

"Rob is high-up in the Police Force," Shania enlightened Leah, "And has worked the past two years on Christmas Day. You can imagine how awful last Christmas was for the emergency services?" Leah nodded, though secretly did not wish to even think about her own last painful and lonely Christmas.

Twenty minutes later, Shania led Leah up the stairs to one of the two guest bedrooms, each with its own small private bathroom. The room, in keeping with the rest of the house, had white walls. A beautiful floral thick-piled rug lay upon the old polished floorboards and the windows were adorned with feminine floral drapes with old-fashioned rope holdbacks and antique brass hooks.

Shania placed Leah's overnight bag carefully upon the high Victorian style brass and iron bed, made up with cotton bedding that matched the pattern and colours of the curtains. There was also a Victorian burr walnut wardrobe with a matching dressing table which had a mirror and a square velvet floral upholstered stall. A pair of matching walnut bedside cabinets displayed the attractive table lamps which had floral motifs burnt into the surface and modern white shades.

"So, if you need anything, I am in the guest bedroom next door to you and Mac is on the top floor in the Main Bedroom. Will you be okay?" asked Shania, as she walked over to the window and pulled the curtains together.

"Yes, thank you so much," Leah said, as she gave her friend a hug, "See you in the morning."

Left alone, Leah unpacked her bag then took her toiletries into the white tiled bathroom. It had a modern white shower suite and blue fluffy towels hung on a heated towel rail. A modern blue washable bathroom mat lay upon the cold floor tiles. She was feeling happily tired and decided to have a warm relaxing shower before going to bed.

Having dried her hair, a few minutes later, with the dryer she had thankfully discovered in a drawer, since she had forgotten to bring her own, Leah was sat up comfortably in the bed, wearing her new purple pyjamas and smelling of her delicious vanilla and coconut scented body and hair wash. She smiled and stretched before snuggling down into the deep springy pillows and soft warm duvet. Within minutes she fell into a peaceful sleep.

Leah awoke the following morning as the smell of delicious cooking filled her nostrils. She reached for her charging phone on the bedside cabinet beside her and noticed the time was seven-thirty.

She thought of her parents, Pam and William, "Happy Christmas, Mum and Dad. I miss you so much," she whispered.

Leah quickly washed, applied her make-up and dressed into smart black trousers, a sparkly red top and her boots, she then fastened a gold necklace with a red pendent, her parents had given her three Christmases before, then took the two cards and small festively-wrapped gifts from her bag and headed downstairs.

Leah found Shania and Mac blissfully happy, working together preparing food in the kitchen area, while listening to old Christmas songs. They smiled and Mac turned the volume of the music down as she approached them.

"Happy Christmas!" Leah wailed and handed them her cards and the two small gifts.

Shania and Mac wished her the same, with hugs and gratitude on opening their well-received presents. Then Shania gave Leah a large awkward parcel wrapped in red shiny paper and tied with a golden bow. Inside she found a new carrycase for her guitar. It was made from a strong fabric and embossed with colourful mythical creatures. It had a strong padded handle and shoulder strap plus a secure pocket for the devices she used to write and record her songs.

"It is absolutely beautiful! It is incredible! Thank you so, so much!" she cried.

Shania had prepared coffee and warm croissants with creamy butter and strawberry jam and the three friends decided to enjoy their breakfast together in the living area.

"What can I do to help?" Leah asked, as they later headed back to the kitchen.

"If you could prepare the salad and fresh fruit cocktail, that would be great?" replied Shania, "Everything that should be in the oven, is in it! Mac will be preparing the various sauces and gravies."

Mac looked surprised by this statement, but dutifully replied, "Yes, that is exactly what I was about to do!" He smiled jokingly at Leah, while Shania playfully rolled her eyes.

Minutes after completing her task and clearing away, Leah felt excited and a little nervous as the first guests arrived. Stephen and Gemma, wearing jeans and *His and Her* Christmas jumpers, handed Shania some chocolates and wine, then made themselves comfortable on a white sofa.

Shortly after, Leah's hopes and excitement plummeted as Taylor entered, looking smart but casual in blue jeans and a navy-blue jumper worn over a soft green silk shirt emphasizing his pleasing green eyes, but was, however, followed inside by an attractive young woman. With straightened long blonde hair tied in a ponytail high on her head, she looked stunning in a tight-fitting red velvet dress revealing her well-toned body and perfect skin. She was so pretty it did not matter that she had applied little make-up; even her fingernails were unpainted and perfectly natural. Leah felt her heart sink; Taylor was a very handsome young man, *of course he must have a girlfriend! Why hadn't the thought entered her mind before?*

On seeing Leah, the young woman smiled and warmly wished her a *Very Happy Christmas* then added, "It is lovely to meet you. I have really been looking forward to today." Leah had to admit it, as her mother would have once said, *this beauty was as lovely on the inside as she was on the outside.*

Taylor looked over at Leah, smiled and winked. *I cannot believe it! He is flirting with me!* She thought angrily, *he doesn't deserve such a nice girlfriend!*

Taylor was a little confused when Leah chose to ignore him so he continued to look at her while seating himself comfortably at one end of the sofa, next to *the beauty* and opposite her own seat of choice, the Edwardian carved, gilded red velvet uphol-stered side chair.

A few seconds later, Jaz appeared wearing brightly coloured leg-gings and a festive t-shirt.

"Hi everyone! Happy Christmas and all of that stuff!" she called out and sat herself down, on the other side of Taylor's sofa.

It was becoming louder in the room, with different voices hold-ing numerous conversations together at the same time. Last to arrive were Howard and Zoe.

Howard entered first, with his thick mop of brown and grey hair and wearing a brown suit that looked a size too large, a beige open necked shirt and well-worn comfortable brown leather loafers. Smiling around at everyone there, while scanning the room with his big green eyes, he fixed them upon Leah and then walked directly over to her.

"Wonderful to finally meet you," he said. "Shania has told me so much about you, Leah, I feel I know you already."

Leah felt a little embarrassed since Shania had said so little about *him*.

At that moment, Zoe entered the noisy room, dressed in an attractive smart beige woollen dress, matching shoes and gold jewellery. Her dark wavy hair was loose and hung to just below her shoulder, her make-up and nails had been perfectly applied as always.

The excitement and racket escalated as Shania announced loudly, "Could you please make your way to the table, where dinner is served!"

With people rushing to wash their hands and deciding where they wanted to sit, Leah refrained from leaving her seat until everyone else was settled.

She was devastated when Shania called out to her, "Come and sit here, Leah, next to Taylor."

Feeling embarrassed and self-conscious, Leah did as she was told. However, she was thankful to have Shania seated on her other side. Once everyone was quiet, Howard offered a short *blessing* of the food.

Everyone joined their hands upon the table. Whilst they had their heads bowed, Leah was outraged when she felt Taylor squeeze her hand tightly. She could not stop herself from immediately looking indignantly up at him. *And with his girlfriend sat right opposite too!* However, *she - the beauty,* also looked up at that very same moment and actually saw Taylor squeeze Leah's hand again, but then ... she simply smiled at them both!

The *blessing* had been said and everyone was helping themselves to the delicious Christmas feast. Jaz leaned across the table to take a slice of the Vegan Loaf.

"Do you want to try some of this Rob? It's really good!" she asked *the beauty*,

"No, you're alright, Jaz, I'll stick to my turkey thanks!" Rob replied and they both laughed, while looking lovingly into one another's eyes.

Watching Leah closely, Taylor then whispered into her ear, "Robyn and Jaz are a great couple, aren't they?"

Leah felt stupid, ignorant and ashamed. She looked round at Taylor's kind face, smiling back at her.

"Yes," she replied, placing her hand on top of his, "Yes, they are. They make a lovely couple."

The table looked incredible, offering numerous dishes; there were various vegetables cooked in assorted sauces, the colourful salad that Leah had prepared, a tray of carved sliced meats as well as a Vegan Mushroom and Lentil Loaf covered with cranberries. It all looked and would surely taste, divine.

Mac began explaining the different gravies, sauces and dishes; which ones were meat-free, and in fact, proved to be the most tasty and popular with everyone.

Leah was enjoying some spiced roasted cauliflower with herbed rice and a large spoonful of the stuffed pumpkin dish, when she suddenly locked eyes with Zoe, whom she had not really noticed until that moment. Leah felt hot and feverish, *maybe she had overeaten and should save some room for the scrumptious desserts soon to be on offer?* She drank some water.

"Taylor," Zoe called across the table, "You have not introduced me to your friend."

"This is Leah ... Shania's flat-mate?" Taylor replied, loudly enough to be heard above the various conversations being held around the table.

Leah smiled at Zoe but was baffled by Zoe's strange response.

"Everyone has been referring to her as *Shania's flat-mate*. I do not recall anyone mentioning her name was Leah?"

The others had begun to quieten down and were watching, appearing slightly awkward and confused. Howard was becoming embarrassed by his wife's odd and rude behaviour.

"Well," he said smiling, "Now you know that Shania's friend is called Leah. Do you want any more wine, Darling?"

Zoe completely ignored Howard and continued to glare at Leah.

"Where have you moved here from?" she probed icily.

Leah felt uncomfortable and exposed. With all eyes upon her, she responded, "I grew up in a place called Leigh-on-Sea in Essex, up until my parents died. Do you know of it?"

Zoe's blood ran cold, realising she had once concealed a terrible secret from her husband that had now returned to haunt her.

Calm and composed, she said, "Yes. I know of it. I am sorry to hear about your parents. I hope you will enjoy your stay here in Lincolnshire."

"Thank you," Leah replied. "I have decided to make Lincoln my home now."

Zoe smiled and excused herself. Once alone in the small downstairs cloakroom, she washed her hands and wrists under the cold tap and glared back at herself in the mirror.

"How do you protect her now?" she asked her reflection, then closed her eyes, "How can I protect her, Rose?"

Conversations had resumed when Zoe returned unnoticed to her place at the table. Colourful desserts of sweet pastries, fresh fruit, puddings and cream were being served.

It was later, when Mac and Shania were serving the coffee, Leah began to feel light-headed. She sipped her water and stared outside into the garden. Suddenly she noticed the frost covered jagged branches of an old cherry tree, swaying in the cold night breeze. She was aware of the roots, thick and twisted, remaining steadfast and solid beneath the hard, frozen ground. She felt a soft rhythm flow through her body and remembered a song she had recently composed. The drum and base beats vibrated gently inside of her chest while the warm relaxing sounds of an acoustic guitar and keyboard played the melody softly inside her mind. Her soul felt light and free, just like the trees and plants outside. She was suddenly oblivious to where she was and of those around her.

Leah's mind took her to other places, other times; to a hut, where a young mother was caring for her small dark haired son ... she watched the boy witness the murder of his people ... then, he had grown into a young man, a soldier ... no! He was different now! She saw the same young man talking to a monk in a small hidden place within a Monastery ... next, he was on a ship, watching a funeral ... then ... he was inside a modern-day house – a mansion. He was wearing a uniform and entering a long conference room. Leah could see the faces of the individuals sat around the conference table ... then ... oh no! Now the same handsome young man, wearing jeans, a woollen sweater and leather jacket was walking towards her, coming ... closer ... closer ...

Leah was suddenly aware of soft concerned voices. She opened her eyes to find herself lying on one of the cream leather sofas. Shania was stroking her forehead, while the others had gathered around her.

The following morning, when Leah awoke in Mac's pretty guest bedroom, she would not remember the fear in the eyes of everyone sat around the table, when she had suddenly gently slipped down from her chair, onto the floor with symptoms of a fever. How Taylor had so carefully and tenderly carried her to the comfort of the soft sofa and how Shania had quickly appeared with a cold wet flannel for her brow. She would not recall the words she had spoken and the things she had revealed, nor the panic in their faces as certain items in the room suddenly began moving - leaping from their place, and Howard's excitable voice asking Shania,

"My God! Has anything like this ever happened before?"

"No! It's only been a fever followed by the revelations!" Shania had answered fearfully.

It was Stephen who had then suggested placing the ancient relics that had fallen from their places, gently into Leah's hand and to their disbelief yet euphoria, received instruction, clarification and meaning for each one.

"Wow! This is terrifying, yet incredible! We seem to have our own Oracle!" Howard had announced.

Zoe had watched in horror as the events of the day had escalated. Now she knew beyond any doubt that Leah's destiny had clearly sent her to them, just as years before, her own had led her to Howard. She knew everything was out of her control. Something greater than all of them, had a plan and it was leading them to something unknown.

For Leah, the following few days were enjoyable, spending time with her two best friends, just chilling in front of the television – although, she did regret indulging in quite so much rich food and drink on Christmas Day, because she had been suffering from a terribly sore head!

Across The Atlantic Ocean, Many Miles Away, In A Remote Area Of Columbia ...

Zachariah had been summoned to report to Raama's luxurious home. His rusting patrol car had driven along the hot, dry rugged road for what had seemed like hours. The scenery dramatically improved within every second of distance travelled on the approach to the impressive white villa. It had an Ancient Greek appearance and was surrounded by luscious green gardens and gleaming white statues.

Zachariah parked his car outside the front steps leading up to the main entrance, as he had done many times before. Today, surprisingly, the side of the property appeared to have its own exclusive carpark, due to the unusual number of expensive vehicles parked there.

A large sweaty suited man, wearing a gun and holder, poorly concealed inside his jacket, approached him,

"Well, if it isn't our own dear Sergeant Garcia! We are so honoured to have you visit us."

Zachariah, ignoring the man and his sarcasm, began ascending the steps. *Sweaty* followed, continuing to mock him.

"We are so fortunate to have you protecting us from all those *horrible criminals* out there! It is so reassuring knowing that we have you on *our side!*" His huge stomach wobbled as he laughed at his own pathetic humour.

Zachariah's expression did not alter, "Where is he?" he demanded coldly.

Sweaty was offended. Using his weight and large frame, he blocked the entrance then grabbed Zachariah by the throat, pushed him through the door and slammed him against the wall.

"You piece of scum!" he shouted, "You are nothing but a filthy pig! When the boss is finished with you, Sergeant Gar-c-ia, you will be killed just like all the others!"

Watched by a couple of other suited buffoons, *Sweaty* spat into Zachariah's eye. Then grabbing him tightly by his shoulder and marching him down the long hallway to the door of a large meeting room, *Sweaty* violently pushed the door open using Zachariah's body.

Once inside, Zachariah began scrutinising the scene before him. Bodyguards were stood all around the room. Raama was holding some kind of meeting, with a few unsavoury faces he recognised from his Police Files, who were responsible for most of the crimes in the vast area and it was *his* job to cover-up. They had all turned to look as he was physically slung inside the room and they clearly approved of his rough treatment.

Zachariah looked at those sitting around the long conference table; a large framed man with an Eastern European accent had been speaking about a rival he wanted *dealt with* while smoking a cigar, also smoking a cigar was the thin elegant oriental woman sat next to him. A large attractive African woman was arguing with two Japanese men opposite her and a woman with short spiky black hair, wearing a man's pinstriped suit, was drinking whisky from a flask and staring at the ceiling. Seated closest to Raama were seven other well-known local drug dealers; four men and three women, dressed no differently than the ordinary residents at a marketplace, and looking quite out of place.

Raama, as always, pleased to see Zachariah, called to him, "Ah! Sergeant Garcia! I was not expecting you until tomorrow. Nice of you to have come early." Turning to the others he laughed, "Our Police Officers here in Columbia are so … helpful and punctual!" There were sniggers.

Zachariah had driven many miles, leaving the job he enjoyed most days. He played his part well as a law enforcer when he could, of course. He resented being reminded of *who* and *what* he really was, whenever Raama summoned him.

"Well, I'm here now. What is it that you want, this time?" he demanded.

There was a sudden tense silence as all those present waited and watched to see how Raama, the most successful and feared Crime Lord in the country, would react to being disrespected by this *fool.* They were shocked, mortified when Raama simply laughed.

"What is the matter with you, eh? Has somebody upset you? If it is one of my men, just kill him and be done with it," he said casually.

Everyone gasped as Raama took a knife concealed within his

jacket and threw it swiftly through the air. Zachariah caught it by the blade, *Sweaty* took a step back, fearing the worst and looked around at his *brothers* – none returned eye contact. However, Zachariah immediately threw the knife back at Raama, who also caught it. Raama laughed, while everyone else in the room were left stunned.

"Let me deal with my friends here, then I will explain why I called you, okay?"

"Okay," Zachariah replied wearily.

Even to Zachariah's surprise, Raama suddenly lifted his left hand, as if to brush away a fly and his bodyguards reached for their guns and murdered every single person sat around the conference table.

Then, Raama casually took a gun from under the table and shot every one of his bodyguards!

"Thieving cheats, the lot of you!" he shouted, before shoving the dead body beside him onto the floor and then addressing Zachariah, "Sit down, Zac."

Stepping over the body, Zachariah obeyed and Raama continued, "There is a problem. One of our own was recently successfully eliminated by a group of mortals."

"Really?" Zachariah felt a sudden and intense jolt inside his soul, "But it should not be possible to ..."

Raama crashed his fists down angrily onto the table, breaking it.

"There is a strong opposition growing, against our master's plan. It is a serious threat that requires our immediate attention. We need to *nip this in the bud* before it grows out of control." He paused, then ... "One man! One man!" he yelled furiously, "Has managed to ruin everything! Somehow, he and others have discovered some of the *old ways* to oppose *the plan*. They know truths that they should not know! They have weapons they should not have! Why? How?"

"So where are we headed?" asked Zachariah.

Raama instantly calmed himself, "England," he answered, "That bleak, miserable place, out in the middle of nowhere, we once knew as *Lindum Colonia.* We need to leave for Lincoln now, with every day that passes, this group, this opposition, is becoming stronger."

Raama set a device, hidden behind a picture in the conference room before he and Zachariah left, taking the steps leading down and out of the building. A quick touch on his phone and there was a large and noisy explosion behind them. The lavish villa exploded into rubble, smoke and flames.

"By the way," Raama said to Zachariah, as they walked towards his Range Rover, "Happy Christmas Zac!"

SONGBIRD

L eah had been wishing this day to arrive quickly ever since Christmas Eve, when Lenny had invited her to audition for the band on the first Tuesday of January, at The Forum.

The day had been spent completing coursework for her university studies, whilst in between, watching previous performances of Lenny and the band online.

Leah never let a day pass without singing, or playing her guitar, so she was in fine voice and ready for the challenge ahead. She had chosen her two songs as instructed by Lenny; the first, was one of her own compositions, an upbeat spiritual rocky number, that would hopefully get the musicians behind her, tapping their toes and enjoying the beat. Her second choice of song had been more difficult; at first, she had wanted to show off another one of her own creations, but then a strong desire to perform one of her father's favourite songs, finally won the battle. She had chosen a song and prepared her own personal arrangement to '*Lead With Your Heart*', a ballad sung by The Canadian Tenors, on a c.d. William often played for the family to listen to, during dinner. Her version was not as dynamic, yet just as beautiful in its simpler stripped-back and creative form.

Leah's outfit of choice was black jeans, a short waisted tight-fitted black shimmering jumper and high-heeled black boots. She had taken extra time with her make-up, she was prepared, just in case the audition was being filmed; she dreaded the thought of being remembered, indefinitely, for how she appeared this evening.

Leah's guitar was sat waiting by the door, with copies of the sheet music she had prepared for the band members, placed carefully in the useful pocket of her new cherished guitar case. Shania had arranged that she and Mac would collect Leah from their flat, on the way to The Forum, killing two birds with one stone; Leah goes for her audition and they attend their ... *Martial Arts Class.*

Shania's text alerted Leah that she and Mac had arrived and were waiting outside in the car. Leah grabbed her winter coat and threw her bag over her shoulder before picking up the guitar case and heading out the door.

Once inside the warmth of Mac's car, Leah noticed the black gym clothing both Shania and Mac were wearing. She thought how smart and attractive they appeared and remembered her one attempt at a 'Clubbercise Class' a few years back and how *she* had looked wearing her new baggy grey sweatpants, sports bra and clingy top. She smiled remembering how difficult it had been for her and Pam, to get that tight stretchy top off! She doubted Shania had ever experienced *that* trouble, then smiled again, visualising Mac pulling the end of Shania's top, whilst Shania's head and arms remained caught up inside – like the meat inside a tight-skinned sausage!

"You look happy," Shania had been observing Leah, smiling thoughtfully to herself, in the mirror.

Leah returned to the real world, "Yes," she said, "I am, and so excited about tonight ... nervous ... but excited!"

Mac parked the car and the three entered The Forum.

"Do you want us to come down to the Main Hall with you?" Shania asked.

"No, thank you. I will be fine." Leah replied.

Shania and Mac headed upstairs to their *class*, while Leah walked slowly and confidently towards the Main Hall, where the door had been left open. Taking a deep breath and whispering to herself, '*Come on, you can do this. Make Mum and Dad proud,*' she entered.

The stage was lit with a soft orange coloured light. The musicians and vocalists were in their positions, quietly chatting to one another. Lenny appeared from backstage, had a quick word with the drummer and then walked to his place, centre stage. He looked up and noticed Leah, stood waiting at the back of the hall, as if waiting for permission to enter the proceedings, *he liked her already.*

"Hi Leah! If you want to get yourself up on stage, we will do your audition first. Don't worry about setting your guitar up, just use mine as it's all ready to play," he instructed.

Leah moved speedily to the stage, placing her coat, bag and guitar case on a seat at the front row.

The performers were now silent, and Leah felt nervous and exposed as she attempted to climb the steps leading up onto the stage, but then she remembered she needed her sheet music from her guitar case. So, pretending to shoot out her own brains with her hands shaped like a pistol, she quickly turned around and headed back to her guitar case, with everyone now watching her curiously, while she found the sheets of paper.

As Leah finally walked onto the stage her footsteps seemed loud and heavy. A sudden beam of white glaring light was pointed directly onto her, the spotlight now following her every move. She handed Lenny, who was wearing a headset microphone, her sheet music and he began distributing it to the band while she took one of two guitars from a stand. Carefully adjusting the strap on her shoulder, then tweaking the height of the microphone stand she now looked up into the spotlight and out into the black auditorium.

"Which one are we starting with, Leah?" Lenny asked.

"'*It's a Great Way*', please." Leah replied, a little shakily.

There was a rustling sound coming through the speakers as the band members sorted their sheet music.

"I don't know this one, who is it by?" Lenny asked.

"Er, I wrote it," she replied, nervously.

"Great," he said, though Leah was not sure whether he meant it, or if he was being sarcastic.

Leah took a deep breath and it was picked up by the microphone. Silence ... then, ... the drummer counted the band in, using his drumsticks. Leah heard and felt the rocky yet soulful rhythm of the keyboards and guitars, as they played the intro. Once she had sung the first few opening lines ...

Are you finding it hard, to make things right?

Would you rather walk away, than take on the fight?

I have news for you, better listen well ...

It's a brand-new day and I've a story to tell.

Leah had lost her nerves and was now loving every second of her experience. The others were too. Her song was fun and cheerful and by the end of it, everyone would be humming the chorus inside their heads for days to come.

Leah then sang her second choice of song, the ballad, '*Lead With Your Heart*'. The simple arrangement with the varied and tender tones of Leah's voice, expressing the meaningful lyrics, sent shivers down the spines of all those fortunate enough to hear it. On finishing the song, a moment of silence ensued as, no one really wanted this experience, which seemed personal to each and every individual, to end.

Having completed her audition, Lenny spoke to Leah in front of the band.

"I am happy to let you join us if you so wish to," he said, "You have a good voice, not the greatest I have ever heard, but you certainly have *something.* You're not a bad rhythm guitarist either, certainly not a lead though. Oh, and I liked your own composition too," he added, matter-of-factly.

The band members clapped and cheered, and Leah put her hands together as if to pray, "Thank you, so much," she said, "I am really thrilled, and grateful!"

A few of the band members stepped forward to congratulate her on her performance and to welcome her to their group.

"Right then, *people!*" Lenny announced, "Back to rehearsals!" He handed Leah a bundle of sheet music saying, "This is what we are practising tonight and I will send you a lot more of the stuff we do, if you could jot down your email address before you leave? Use my guitar tonight, let's save some time – but stand back there, please."

He pointed to a spot between a guitarist and keyboard, then informed her, "I always have two guitars on stage, anyway."

Leah took her spot on the stage and could feel a sense of pride and belonging. The evening went well and to her surprise Lenny even asked Leah to sing the lead in one of the new songs they were to practise for the first time. It was a new experience for her to sing with such talented and experienced musicians and the wonderful voices of the backing singers overwhelmed her senses. She was blissfully happy and eager to tell Shania and Mac all of her news later.

When rehearsals were over, each band member introduced themselves to Leah before leaving and she was part of a few light conversations before she was free to go over to Lenny and give him her email address.

"Thank you," he said, taking the leaflet which, she had given to him, with her email written on the back. "Before you go, could I have a quick word?"

"Yes, of course," she replied.

"That second song you sang for your audition, I would like to include it in our music for this week's Sunday Service. You don't need to come here on Sunday, if you don't want to, but would you be free on Friday night to come along and sing it again, for the camera?"

Leah felt ecstatic yet terrified, at the same time. "Yes, I would love to," she replied.

"Okay, we get here for around seven. See you then." And with this, Lenny left, leaving Leah wondering whether the previous few wonderful hours had *really just happened.*

Feeling tired yet content, Leah made her way down to the entrance and stood waiting. A few people passed her, coming out from the various rooms upstairs. She decided to move her guitar case, coat and bag to a more sensible and unobtrusive place a few paces away. She was extremely surprised and happy, to then see Taylor suddenly appear. He was sweating and she recognised his training clothes as the same style that Shania and Mac had been wearing.

"Hello Taylor!" she said, taking him by surprise.

"Leah!" he exclaimed, then smiling brightly, "Of course, it is Tuesday! You had your audition with Lenny and the band tonight! How did it go?"

Before Leah had the opportunity to reply, Stephen, Gemma and Jaz, all came down the stairs together. They were dressed in their everyday attire; however, their hair was noticeably wet from sweat. Then Shania appeared, followed by Mac, who had also changed out of their training clothes.

"I didn't realise you all attended Jaz's Martial Arts Class!" Leah said, having finished her '*Hello*'s.

They all looked at one another as Shania began to explain awkwardly, "Oh yes, we love Jaz's classes and working out together, don't we?" There were a couple of bewildered and badly acted responses of agreement.

Now, appearing from the stairs was Howard, followed closely

by a group of noisy and excitable young boys and girls and a weary looking young man who was their Tech Teacher.

"Have you had a good time?" Howard asked the little students as they rushed past him.

They all nodded, and one boy named Sebastian replied, "Yes! I have moved up *another* level this week! My dad says I am a tech *genius*!"

"Well," agreed Howard, smiling down at the proud child, "I think your dad is right, Seb."

However, Sebastian's smile was immediately wiped off his face, as a girl with long blonde hair, tied in bunches, announced smugly, "I went up *two* levels, Howard."

"Oh, well done to you as well, Trinity," Howard answered awkwardly.

"Thank you," Trinity said smiling, then turned and pulled a self-satisfied face of superiority at the now scowling Sebastian.

"Right then! Off you all go!" Howard said, hurrying them along. To his relief, a driver appeared through the doorway and addressed the group of excitable children.

"Come on kids! The minibus is waiting to take you home!" A short moment of chaos followed as the children ran noisily outside, then all was calm once more.

Howard noticed Leah among the group.

"Hello Leah! Nice to see you again," he said, as Zoe was now coming down the stairs.

On seeing Leah, Zoe's smile faded, though only Leah noticed, as everyone else had begun saying their farewells.

On the journey back, by the time it took for Leah to joyfully tell Shania and Mac everything that had happened with Lenny, Mac had dropped them both off, home.

"Are you not staying at Mac's tonight?" enquired Leah.

"No, I need to be at work early tomorrow, just across from The Brayford," Shania replied.

Shania, feeling particularly fatigued this evening after Jaz's strenuous and exhausting training session, decided to go straight into the bathroom to have a shower before bed. She had wearily dropped her training bag by the front door on entering their flat, so Leah, having just made them both some hot chocolate, noticed it and decided to put it in Shania's room. As she lifted the bag she could see it had not been closed properly and something inside was catching the zipper. It was Shania's black training clothes, so Leah thought she might as well put the washing into their laundry basket.

Having corrected the zipper, Leah lifted out the clothing, but something else, something unusual at the bottom of the bag, caught her eye.

Looking similar to a woven crepe fabric, it was black, sparkly and it twinkled in the light. Curiously, she touched it, softly running her fingers under a layer of the pliable materiel. However, she jolted away from it, terrified at the sudden consequence of the fabric having just touched her skin. For it moved independently, having a will of its own. The small piece of fabric she had touched had expanded, growing into rigid tiny scales, yet it was similar to leather, appearing lithe and flexible. On withdrawing her flesh from the bag, the hard yet compliant materiel immediately returned to its original state, a small soft twinkling ripple of cloth.

Leah could not believe what she had just encountered. Fear consumed her and she sat staring into the bag for a few stunned moments.

Leah heard Shania close the shower door, so quickly folded the cloth and training clothes back into the bag and replaced it to where Shania had left it, by the front door.

She called out to Shania, "I've made you a hot chocolate and it's on the coffee table! I am off to bed now. Goodnight!"

"Oh, okay then, thank you," Shania replied, as she entered the living room, still drying her long, wet hair with a towel and wearing her silk dressing gown. She was just in time to see Leah's door close behind her.

Friday

The following few days, Leah decided she had no choice other than to put her experience with the contents of Shania's bag, to the back of her mind. She could not make any sense of it and had begun questioning whether she had just been tired and had imagined the whole thing. After all, it would not be the first time that weird and unexplainable things had randomly entered her mind recently.

Leah had completed some coursework while Shania had been kept busy with her ever-growing workload, so she and Leah had not seen much of one another since Tuesday, the night of Leah's audition. However, tonight Mac was collecting them both once again, to take them to The Forum.

Stood, waiting outside for Mac's car to arrive, Shania asked Leah, "Are you okay? You aren't nervous are you? You look great tonight, by the way."

Leah smiled, "I am good, thank you. Yes, I am nervous and … I hope I do look alright, because **you** helped me to pick the clothes I am wearing!"

They were both laughing as Mac pulled up and they scrambled into the car.

On arriving at The Forum, Shania and Mac immediately went upstairs while Leah headed, with her guitar to the Main Hall.

Band members were still arriving and setting up their instruments, another musician had been added to the line-up tonight, a professional music-stand held his saxophone, flute and clarinet. The stage looked beautiful, with different coloured lighting incorporating a soft atmospheric haze.

Outside, Zachariah had already driven the new black Range Rover he had bought on first entering the United Kingdom, into the carpark of The Forum.

Raama had sat in the passenger seat giving instructions.

"Park at the back, behind those cars, over there and we won't be so noticeable," he ordered.

Zachariah did as he was told then asked, "So, what is the plan tonight?"

Raama thought for a moment, then, "We need information and answers before we do anything. So, today we are simply two strangers wishing to learn more about *this amazing place that everyone is speaking about.*"

They left the car and headed towards the entrance, where a group of youths, dressed in tracksuits, scarves and gloves, had just emerged, one was holding a basketball. Raama and Zachariah stopped and watched the teenagers head to round the side of the building where there was a designated sports court with powerful outside overhead lighting.

Zachariah looked handsome in his jeans, a warm navy-blue woollen sweater and black leather jacket and boots. Raama, was dressed similarly in jeans, but wore a thick winter's coat. Both men had dark hair, dark eyes and complexions, however, Zachariah was the more attractive and younger looking out of the two.

Zachariah took the first couple of steps leading up into the building and stopped when he noticed that Raama had remained stood at the bottom. Two young women smiled as they passed them and headed inside. Raama was charming and acknowledged them, whereas Zachariah, to the girls' disappointment, had ignored them.

"What's the matter?" Zachariah asked Raama, quietly.

"Come back down here and I will tell you," Raama uttered incensed, clenching his teeth. He began walking back to their car, followed by Zachariah.

"So?" asked Zachariah, "What is the problem?"

"I cannot enter the place," Raama continued, "Very clever, very clever indeed. You will have to go in alone."

"What do you mean, you cannot enter? It is not built on *sacred ground*, is it?" Zachariah was mystified.

"No, it is not," Raama acknowledged thoughtfully, "They have clearly used stones from *the old place* during its construction. There are also other strong forces flowing through its walls. I cannot go further than the perimeter, but luckily, you can because you are of *mortal birth*."

Zachariah had earlier noticed a beautiful young woman, getting out of a car with two other mortals. She had long wavy dark brown hair and a face that captivated him the first second he saw her. This was a new experience for him, and he was bewildered at his own undeniably strong attraction towards her as he had watched her climb the steps, carrying her guitar in its colourful case. He now felt impatient to follow her inside.

Once again, Zachariah walked slowly and purposely up the steps to The Forum. Nobody was around to question him as he entered the building so he immediately headed in the direction of which he could hear and sense life.

Finding himself in a dark and now silent theatre, with musicians standing and dramatically waiting quietly on the atmospheric stage, he took a seat at the far back, completely unnoticed.

The stage was black, then ... mist and bewitching lights lit up the musicians as the keyboard player, followed by the bass, began to play a haunting melody. Then he saw *the girl* again; the most exquisite soul, walk slowly onto the stage, in a surrounding pillar of white light. She was wearing a delicate lacy, autumn-coloured floral blouse, that revealed her slim tantalizingly long neckline. She wore black trousers, the same as the band, though they were all dressed completely in black. Her brown soft shiny curls moved as she did and her face was *angelic yet mysterious.* Her character revealed a feminine gentleness and serenity, together with a strength, confidence and purpose.

On reaching the microphone stand, placed in the centre of the stage, Leah looked out into the blinding spotlight and the darkness surrounding it and sang the first few enthralling lines of her song. Her previous nerves and insecurity from having Lenny tell her not to use her beloved guitar this evening, had now disappeared.

The first part of the song was soft, tranquil and calmed the soul. As more instrumental joined in the subtle build-up of the melody and Leah's hypnotic voice, effortlessly reached the higher notes, expressing and feeling the meaning of the lyrics, Zachariah was bewitched. Every part of his being, yearned to be alone with this young woman; to touch her face and hair, to kiss her lips, hold her in his arms and to protect her with every part of his tormented body and soul.

As Leah performed the song her father, William, had once enjoyed listening to with his family, Leah felt herself surrounded by love. She thought of the many lessons her parents had installed into her and the protected but happy life, she had once known. Tonight, she felt different ... altered ...

Somehow, something deep inside of herself was telling her, that a new and exciting chapter of her life, was about to begin.

Leah looked through the heavenly spotlight, out into the darkness of the Main Hall and could feel a strong force. An unexplainable energy was fiercely, burning into her very soul. Suddenly, she felt stronger ... *special.*

Though she could not see Zachariah, sitting at the far back of the hall, Leah sang to him. Inadvertently, she messed with his thoughts, his soul and his heart.

At the end of the spellbinding performance, the lights were switched back on in the theatre. Lenny walked forward from his position on the stage, a few paces away from Leah.

"Thank you, Leah, that was great," he said, "That is all I need from you tonight, so you are free to go now." Then, "Are you ready, *ladies*?"

With this, Lenny looked down into the first row of seats, where a group of three woman, aged in their mid-forties had been sat. Dressed in matching attractive black skirts and turquoise blouses, they now stood up and made their way up on to the stage. Each one congratulated Leah on her *moving* performance as she passed them.

Leah had finished earlier than she had expected to, so leaving her guitar in the hall, she took her coat and bag, deciding to get some fresh air outside. For she knew Mac and Shania would not be finishing for a while yet.

As Leah walked past Suzie and Phil, the two young technicians, busily preparing to film the next vocal performers, she smiled and then headed out of the doors of the Main Hall. She had noticed Zachariah. Though their eyes had met for only a fraction of a second, a bolt of thunder had just shattered her insides! She felt shaky and excited. Her heart missed a beat when she noticed him stand and follow her outside.

Feeling slightly dry and breathless, Leah stopped at one of the vending machines and bought herself a cold drink before sitting down at one of the tables close by, where she thirstily consumed half of it within seconds.

"Would you mind if I joined you?" came a strong, husky and masculine voice. Leah looked up at Zachariah.

"Hello, I am Zac," he said.

Leah had never in her life, experienced such a strong and overwhelming emotion upon meeting a stranger, nevertheless, she was somehow able to take a deep breath, compose herself and appear calm.

She smiled and answered, "Yes, of course. Hi, my name is Leah. Are you a member here?"

Zachariah did not want to lie to her.

"No, I was just curious about the place ... and the people," he continued, not wanting to break their intense eye-contact for one second, "Are you a member, Leah? Could you enlighten me?"

Leah thought for a moment, then replied, "I am quite new here myself, actually, but I have found the place to be extremely spiritual ... fun ... educational ..."

Zachariah interrupted her, "What about the leader ... the pastor? Do you know him?"

Leah's face lit up, "Oh yes! The pastor, Howard, is extremely nice and his wife is beautiful. I have made a few good friends here; my flatmate, Shania and her boyfriend – well, fiancé actually, they belong to the church. Oh, and they go to the Martial Arts Classes."

"Martial Arts?" he quizzed.

"Yes, they teach all sorts of subjects here!" Leah said.

"Where are they now? Are they somewhere, having *a class*?"

As Zachariah asked the question, he felt someone standing behind him and then noticed Leah give whoever it was, a warm and genuine smile. He turned his chair to find a handsome young man, dressed in jeans and a sweater, looking down sternly at him with his unmistakable green eyes. He appeared breathless and was sweating, clearly having recently executed some form of strenuous exercise.

He spoke, ignoring Zachariah, "Hi, Leah. Is everything alright?"

Leah replied, feeling a little embarrassed by Taylor's chilly attitude, "Yes, thank you. I have finished my bit with Lenny for this evening. This is Zac, Taylor. He wants to know more about The

Forum. Maybe you could help him?"

Taylor turned his attention to Zachariah. "Well ... Zac ... we have a really good website, explaining all the courses we run here."

Zac interrupted, "Well, it is strange that you should say that Taylor, since I guess you and Leah's friends, have been somewhere doing your ... Martial Arts Class ... yet, funnily enough ... *that ... activity ...* is not advertised on your social media for this evening?"

The two men locked angry eyes on one another. The air was tense and volatile. Leah felt nervous.

Zac smiled at Taylor, making him inwardly seethe,

"Anyway, Taylor, maybe you could enlighten me about your great pastor, Howard ... that was the name you said, wasn't it, Leah?"

"Yes, that's right," Leah replied, aware something unpleasant was going on between these men and that she had just been used as a trigger, to further agitate Taylor.

"I could do with making a few spiritual changes in my life. Maybe this place could help me?" Zac taunted him further.

Taylor was fuming and finding the strong urge to strike out at Zac increasingly more difficult to repress, by the second.

However, to Leah's relief, Stephen, Mac and Jaz, now arrived at the table. Like Taylor, they had changed into their ordinary clothes and pulled up chairs for themselves. Mac was forced to practically hug Taylor, to get him seated.

"Leah, you must introduce us to your new friend!" Mac said, smiling at both her and Zac.

Leah obliged, "This is Zac and ..."

Before, she could say any more, Stephen interrupted, "In *these times*, people usually contact us before just turning up, Zac. We have many varied activities to offer, not all are advertised, but I am sure we could find something to interest you if you are genuinely interested. And if it is spiritual guidance you are seeking, then we have many volunteers who can help you to ... find peace."

Taylor then added, repugnantly, "Yes, I would be happy to volunteer to give him ... peace."

Zac laughed, as Mac commented, "You must forgive Taylor, he is very protective of The Forum and of its members. It is not a good idea to antagonise him. Those who have, have deeply regretted it."

Zac turned to look at Taylor again and asked dryly, "What did you do, Taylor, *unfriend them* on social media?"

As Taylor jumped off his seat, Stephen quickly moved in between him and Zac, creating a barrier. He forcefully sat Taylor down once more.

Jaz spoke, "It is time you left now, Zac."

"And don't you come back here!" seethed Taylor.

Zac smiled at the group, then looked at Leah as he stood, "It was nice meeting you, Leah. I don't think your friends like me very much, so I will be going now. Goodbye."

Leah remained quiet, as her mind was in turmoil. She was confused and upset by her friends' hostility towards this stranger, while she had a strong desire to get to know more about him. In truth, a *desire to be with him.*

All would have ended there, if Taylor had only kept his mouth tightly closed, but instead, "He is going down!" Followed by, "Don't worry Leah, I won't let him near you again."

The others raised their eyebrows, frustrated with their friend and now expecting the consequences.

Leah, furious while remaining composed, stood, looked indignantly back at Taylor and replied, "You were extremely rude, Taylor and I am quite capable and free, to choose my own friends."

With this, Leah walked away from the group and picked up one of the information leaflets on her way outside, where Zac had just headed.

Jaz shook her head, looking directly at Taylor, she muttered sarcastically, "Well done, *Mr Darcy*."

Zac was outside, striding across the carpark, heading towards his car, when he heard Leah calling him. He turned and was concerned to find she had followed him.

"I am so sorry about Taylor; he is not usually so rude," she said apologetically. "Here, this is a leaflet with some information about The Forum."

At that moment, Zac's worst fear transpired, as he heard Raama's voice from behind him.

"Well, Zac, you must introduce me to your friend."

Not giving Zac an opportunity to respond, Leah initiated their introduction.

"Hello, I am Leah. I have a leaflet for Zac to have a look at, it gives information about what is offered here at The Forum."

Then she looked back at Zac, "There are places left for the second Worship Meeting on Sunday, if you are free? I am going, I could book you a seat?"

Reluctantly, removing her gaze from Zac's dark eyes, she then addressed Raama, "Of course, you are welcome to come too?"

Raama smiled, charmingly, "It is genuinely nice to meet you, Leah. I am Zac's brother ... he calls me R and please, you must do the same. Thank you so much for your kind invitation. Sadly, I have a previous engagement, but I know Zac is available and so eager to learn more. What time should he meet you here?"

Leah turned and looked searchingly at Zac, who was now staring down at the ground.

"Well," she began, "How about I meet you outside the entrance at ten minutes to eleven, Zac?"

"He will be here," Raama smiled, graciously. He then turned and headed towards their car.

Zac now looked once more into her mesmerising and trusting eyes. There was so much he wanted to say; so many things to warn her about. Instead, he just smiled slightly and nodded.

"Take car, Leah," he said.

Leah's thoughts were also in turmoil, bewildered by these strong feelings Zac had ignited inside of her.

Feeling braver and responding more forwardly than she had ever done so before, she added, "I am really pleased to have met you, Zac. I am so looking forward to seeing you again on Sunday. Don't be late, will you?"

Leah walked away and Zac felt a sense of relief as he watched her return, to the safety of The Forum. He noticed Taylor opening the door and speaking to her. She smiled and gave him a hug. For the first time ever, Zachariah was subjected to yet another new experience, that of *jealousy*.

The following day, Taylor collected Leah from her flat to take her out for lunch. He had used the unpleasant events with Zac to his advantage and talked Leah into a date; *the perfect way to apologise to her for his behaviour the previous evening.*

It was a chilly but bright day, Leah had chosen a warm but stylish white sparkly sweater with black jeans, boots and her smart black winter jacket with a colourful scarf. Taylor wore blue jeans, brown leather desert boots, a beige, chunky, cable-knit sweater and a country-style, brown, tweed shooting jacket.

As Leah jumped inside the passenger seat of Taylor's car, he gave her the warmest of smiles and she could not help but notice how handsome he looked and how divinely he smelt, of dry amber and vanilla.

In less than an hour, Taylor had driven them to Boston. They had made simple chit-chat for the entire journey and were relaxed, enjoying one another's company. Leah found Taylor to be funny, yet intelligent and interesting when debating in more serious conversation. He found her fascinatingly beautiful and grew even fonder of her as the day proceeded.

Together, they explored the Town Centre and enjoyed looking around the Marketplace before going inside the local ancient Church, St Botolph's, endearingly known as *The Boston Stump*. Leah found it fascinating as she and Taylor climbed the 209 steps to the 83m high tower, where on a fine day, views reached far over The Wash and in the opposite direction, to Lincoln Cathedral.

Taylor explained to her, "Leading up to the entrance, is known as the *Puritan Path*. Members of the local congregation, back in the 1630's, were part of those who attempted to establish an English settlement for religious Puritans in New England, North America. Nowadays, known as the City of Boston, Massachusetts. My own ancestors were members of the original congregation."

Later, sitting on a bench in the park, Leah hungrily devoured the tasty hot sausage roll, followed by a delicious cream and jam scone, Taylor had bought them from a small family run baker's shop. Though the temperature was low, the glorious bright sunshine made the air feel warm, fresh and comfortable.

Enjoying their steaming hot, milky, sweet coffee, Leah asked Taylor, "You seem to be extremely close to your uncle. You clearly have a wonderful relationship with Howard and Zoe. Do your parents live in Lincolnshire too, Taylor?"

Taylor took another sip of his coffee, studied Leah for a moment with his intense green eyes, then replied, "I lost both my parents when I was eighteen. I had just started at university when they were involved in a fatal car accident over in the States. I do not know exactly what happened as Howard graciously offered to go and sort everything out over there. Howard and Zoe were fantastic. Howard was ... is, *my rock.* He insisted that I continue my studies and was constantly there for me. I would not have achieved everything I have if it were not for his ... for both of their, love and unconditional support."

Leah took hold of his hand, "I am so sorry, Taylor. Do you have any brothers or sisters?" she asked.

"No, I was an only child. I now run the family business and I live alone in the same house I grew up in. Some day I will raise my own family there," he replied thoughtfully, then added, "I am sorry about your parents too, Leah."

They stared into one another's eyes, understanding and feeling the other's great pain and loss. Leah then attempted to rest her head on his shoulder, however Taylor managed to gently kiss her. It lasted for a few moments and Leah enjoyed the feel of his soft warm lips upon her own. She could smell the coffee on his breath and the wonderful aroma of his scent. They kissed again.

Without warning, a *buzzing* sound coming from Taylor's watch along with a vibration inside the pocket of his jacket, suddenly alarmed them both. They laughed. However, Taylor's happy expression soon changed once he had looked at his phone.

"We need to return to Lincoln as quickly as possible, my uncle has had a break-in," he informed Leah.

On the speedy yet careful journey back to Lincoln, Taylor explained that there was not enough time for him to take her home. They were soon parked in front of Howard and Zoe's Uphill gated property.

"Wait here, Leah," Taylor instructed and ran to the open gate. Leah could see Stephen and Gemma's motorcycles and Mac and Jaz's cars, all randomly parked on the driveway, in front of the house.

Taylor held his breathe as he entered his uncle's home, fearing the worst. He was deeply relieved to find Howard and Zoe standing unharmed, in their trashed lounge, surrounded by the others.

The usually immaculate room, with its brown leather classic Chesterfield Suite, thick-piled green patterned carpet and carved oak cupboard from the court of Queen Elizabeth I, had been the scene of an attempted execution. However, the ingenious and effective alarm system, created by Taylor, had once again, detected a threat which, within seconds, had systematically alerted the knights and prevented a tragedy.

Mac and Jaz were each holding the arm of a young dark-haired boy, aged around fourteen years old. He looked distressed and was attempting to escape their strong hold.

"Sorry, I had to come back from Boston. Leah is waiting in my car outside in the street," Taylor explained.

"Don't worry, Taylor," Shania assured him, "You had told us you would be there with Leah today and anyway; we were able to get here before *this* did any damage." Shania showed Taylor the lethal long razor-edged kitchen knife.

Taylor once more looked at the troubled youth. "I recognise you," he said, "How do think your family will feel after this?"

The boy chose to remain silent.

Stephen then spoke, "I think Mac, Jaz and I need to go and break this to his family. We are well acquainted with them and I know they will be mortified," Adding, "Gemma and Shania, if you could help Howard and Zoe tidy up here and secure the breach, I think Taylor should take Leah home."

Everyone agreed with the plan.

Meanwhile, still waiting nervously outside in Taylor's car, Leah noticed a man dressed in a dark overcoat and a black Fedora hat, walking briskly out of the entrance gate, having walked around the outside of Howard's property. She questioned herself as she thought how he resembled a man she had met the previous day, Zac's brother, R!

Shortly afterwards, Taylor returned to drive her home, unwilling to explain events any further than that, '*Howard and Zoe were fine, having dealt with a young opportunist thief.*'

Leah began to tell him about R, "I think I recognised a man who, I can't be sure, but I think he came out of the garden while you were inside with Howard and Zoe. He might be Zac's brother?"

She was upset by Taylor's frustrated and sarcastic response, "You *think* you recognised him? ... You *think* he came out of the garden?" He shook his head, gave a short cynical laugh, then breathing heavily, bit his lower lip until it bled.

Taylor dropped Leah outside her apartment block, with the atmosphere turning as frosty as the increasingly cold, early evening air.

"Will you be at The Forum tomorrow?" she asked him, as she left his car and stood on the street outside, holding the door open.

"Yes, probably just for the First Service though," he answered abruptly.

Leah waited an awkward moment, hoping he might want to make any future arrangements to see her again, however he did not.

"Well," she said proudly, feeling hurt and annoyed, "I will see you whenever."

With this, she closed the door, rather sharply and Taylor drove away.

ALLIES

J az started the engine of her blue Mini Clubman, while Stephen and Mac manhandled the struggling youth into the back seat. Having strapped him in securely, Mac sat with Jaz in the front, while Stephen remained in the back, glaring icily at their captive.

Minutes later, they arrived outside a grand detached house, in a wealthy and affluent leafy road; surrounded by ancient Silver Birch, Oak and Sweet Chestnut trees.

Jaz drove onto the long driveway and parked as close as possible to the splendid front door. She and Mac immediately vacated the car.

Clearly expecting their arrival, a group of men came out from the house. An elderly man called Sadaat and his eldest son, Naveen, were followed by two younger men in their mid-twenties, Sadaat's youngest son, Rafi, and his friend Eshan.

Each of the men, graciously acknowledged Jaz and Mac, as they waited for Stephen to bring the youth, held tightly by his arm, to stand before them.

Sadaat spoke first, "Thank you, Jaz, Mac and Stephen. I am grateful that you have chosen to hand my grandson over to us, his family, rather than to the police." Then he added, "I have just finished speaking with Howard. Thankfully, he and Zoe, seem to be alright having experienced this horrendous ordeal."

"We were able to prevent a catastrophe for both our communities," Jaz said, handing the deadly looking knife to the boy's father, Naveen. He took it with both hands, almost crying. He turned to his son, searching the young face for any signs of regret. There were none.

"Trust me," Naveen said tearfully, "Believe me when I tell you, that he will be *severely* punished."

Mac then addressed his friends, Eshan and Rafi.

"The boy will need close watching in the future. However, we believe he was indoctrinated by a recent arrival to Lincoln. He was **not** encouraged to do this by anyone within your own community, be reassured. He was clearly manipulated to serve the purpose of those wishing to steer hatred and misunderstanding between our faiths."

Rafi responded, "Yes, now our conflict and hostility are not between men. *Evil* will no-longer be permitted to continue working unnoticed, causing subtle devastation upon the Earth while we are too occupied battling one another."

Eshan then enquired, "Do we know of any other purpose for this attack, was anything stolen from Howard?"

Stephen answered, "We are not sure yet, however, as we recently warned you, we must all be prepared for what is to come."

Rafi stepped forward and added, "We are ready, we will fight together as *Brothers* when the day is upon us."

At that moment, the youth broke free from Stephen's lesser hold and shouted, "Raama is my B*rother*! Not you!" Then he ran inside the house.

Sadaat shouted angrily at his eldest son, "Go and deal with your boy!"

Stephen, Mac and Jaz looked one to the other, then spoke all at once ...

"Raama!" Now they had a name, an important and valuable piece of information.

Naveen, feeling angry and humiliated, stormed back inside, following the resentful steps of his only, infuriating and disappointing offspring.

As Mac and Stephen were returning to the car, Jaz looked at the remaining three men and said sternly, "If the boy is caught anywhere near Howard, Zoe or The Forum in the future, we will have no choice. He will face the same consequences of any other of our enemies."

Sadaat replied wearily, "We understand; you must do what you have to do. However, my grandson will be receiving some serious education and discipline from now on. He will not cause you any trouble again."

The men watched the blue Mini drive away, before Eshan said his farewells to the others.

"Take care, my friends. As-salamu alaykum!" Then he headed towards his white Kia Rio, parked just across the street.

Sunday Morning

Leah had been waiting patiently outside the entrance of The Forum, her phone now said it was five minutes to eleven and Zac still had not arrived. Just as she was about to go inside alone, she noticed the shiny black Range Rover drive into the carpark and stop directly in front of her. She walked slowly down the steps as Zac got out of the driver's seat.

"I am sorry, I kept you waiting," he said, "I have decided that it is best if I do not go inside with you today after all; your friends made it undeniably clear that they don't welcome strangers such as myself. I do not want to cause you anymore trouble. However, I would like to get to know you more. Please ... Leah ... would you come for a coffee with me instead?"

Leah felt a mixture of emotions; excitement at seeing Zac again, anger at the rudeness and hostility her friends had displayed towards him ... and fear.

Was she really prepared to leave with this man she had only recently met and whom she knew nothing about? Her answer was an immediate and surprising ... yes!

A few quiet moments later, Zac drove his car into a carpark, a short distance from The Waterfront. Leah felt relieved and more relaxed as Zac had brought them to a public place. They walked silently together for a few moments before Zac led Leah to a seat which looked out across the water. They observed the boats and swans and enjoyed light conversation. The weather was cold, but sunny and bright, so it was fairly busy with walkers. Friends were noisily meeting up together for breakfast, in the outside areas of the various coffee shops and restaurants.

Zac bought them a coffee from a nearby takeaway kiosk. On returning and giving her the hot milky drink, he seemed tense and uneasy. She could feel summer butterflies dancing inside her stomach as he sat down closely beside her.

"Are you alright?" she asked.

Zac looked at her sweet face and longed to kiss her.

"Yes," he assured her, "I could not be happier. I am, however, just a little mindful that your friends will be ... concerned about you."

"Maybe," Leah replied, "They are good people. It is sad that you and they, did not start off on a sweeter note. They have helped me to build a new and happy life here in Lincoln and I will always appreciate their friendship. However, I will be telling them that they must be much nicer to you in the future."

Her words caused him to laugh, just a little.

Leah stared into Zac's dark eyes and suddenly felt a great sadness there; tragic heart-breaking events, of which those memories still haunted him. When Zac studied the beauty of *her* eyes, he felt an inner-strength and an intense, undeniably strong connection.

Leah had some questions for him that she needed clarifying, "Why did you and 'R' *really* come to The Forum, Zac? Do you really believe in Howard's ideals? Do you even believe there is a God?"

Zac was not prepared for these kinds of discussions, nor his sudden unexpected intention, not to deceive her. He considered his answers carefully before replying.

"I cannot speak for my brother, but I came to The Forum because I wanted to learn more about Howard and his achievements," he said, "He has accomplished so much within a small amount of time. As for God ... it could be so ... Maybe there are many Gods? ... What is the matter, you look surprised?"

Leah *was* surprised. "Well, I expected you to say something like ... *if there was a God, why does He or She allow all the terrible catastrophes; hunger, disease, war, etc, etc,?"*

Zac held her gaze and replied, "Well, the Earth was created with enough land, food, water and medicines for **all** of its inhabitants. I guess God is not to blame when one of the life-forms created, choose to constantly war with one another, each desiring all of the world's resources for themselves ... to disrespect nature and every other living creature ... to devastate lands and oceans. However, I would have more faith if *He* or *She*, chose to do *something* about it, don't you think so, Leah?"

Now it was Leah's turn to once again, consider her own regularly and silently deliberated questions. But then Zac suddenly stood and was offering her his hand, which she warmly accepted.

Holding Zac's hand felt natural and comfortable. They walked along *The Waterfront* and up into the City Centre through *The Hole in the Wall*.

As they began to ascend the hill, walking past various stores, Leah suddenly felt strange; breathless, dizzy, hearing loud voices in her head. Zac felt her body become weak and was able to prevent her from falling, just in time. He scooped his strong arm around her and supported her to a quieter area at the side of a large closed-up department store. A brick ledge surrounded some shrubbery and she was grateful for somewhere private to sit.

Zac studied her carefully, realising she had reacted at the exact same time as they had walked across the High Street where long forgotten, ancient religious sacred stones, lay buried beneath the many layers of time. *Surely, this was no coincidence?*

Leah's head was now spinning and filled with loud angry voices. Suddenly, one particular voice was stronger ... then, everything stopped.

In slow motion, Leah watched an overweight man in his early thirties, with brown skin and soulless eyes, walk straight past them.

Zac was astounded when Leah opened her eyes and took hold of his hand, "That man ... he is intending to kill someone! We must stop him, Zac."

"Are you feeling alright now? Can you walk okay?" he asked her.

"Definitely," she affirmed, "let's go!"

Without hesitation, or further questioning, Zac supported Leah as they began to trail discreetly behind the man.

Moments later, the man, Musad, disappeared through the small narrow alley, *St Peter's Passage*, where he met with four thugs. Following a brief conversation, he handed each of them a white envelope containing money, which they counted before accompanying him to a nearby carpark. Zac and Leah trailed, watching intently from a safe distance.

Ten minutes passed before the smartly dressed, handsome young man, Eshan, appeared and walked across the empty carpark towards his white Kia Rio. The gang pounced like hyenas attacking an unsuspecting fawn, dragging him into an unused corner of the carpark, behind three large recycling bins and out of sight.

Eshan, the innocent victim, began to regain his senses, having just been hit over the head with a large stone by one of the brutes. He was then repeatedly kicked and beaten until Musad instructed the ruffians to cease.

Two of the heavies, lifted Eshan, who was bleeding from his head, nose and mouth, to a standing position. Musad put his bloated face up close to Eshan's.

"I warned you, Eshan, did I not? I told you to keep away from Sabia! She would never have even considered divorcing me! I knew it had to be because of you! Did you think I would just disappear and let you have her?"

Eshan spat blood into his enemy's face.

"You mistreated her and have gotten away with it for far too long! You're an idiot! Sabia came to her senses on her own, she had kept the secret of your cruelty from us all! I haven't even seen her in months!"

Musad smirked, "Are you telling me that you haven't seen how I left her on the day she produced legal documents, ordering me out of my own house? What I did to her before the police arrived? Well," he continued smugly, "Let me tell you this much, the broken glass that she *accidentally* fell on to, will ensure that she never dances again!"

Eshan knew of Sabia's final torment at the hands of Musad and had wanted, as did her brother Rafi, to kill him. However, Sabia had instructed her father, Sadaat, to stop any acts of retribution on her behalf. She had told him from her hospital bed, that it was *her right* to take *her own* vengeance once she was strong enough. (He had assumed by this, that she meant; by taking half of Musad's assets.) Her first concern had been about her beloved and wounded, dog Amir, who had attempted to help his mistress. He had been cruelly restrained with a chocking chain around his neck, tied to a stair bannister, then pitilessly beaten. Sabia had been adamant that Amir be nursed and taken care of by her friend, Zoe, for the duration of her own recuperation.

Though Eshan had been assured of Sabia's remarkable and quick recovery, then of her wishes to be left alone for a while, he was now disgusted, listening to Musad's sick self-gratification. Uncontrollable anger ignited inside his whole body, but he was forcefully restrained and could do nothing.

Another yob, instantly grabbed Eshan's hair, roughly pulling his head backwards. Musad was now brandishing a crude menacing pocket penknife. He placed the thin blade against Eshan's neck, shouting to one of the other men, who was brandishing his phone.

"Make sure you are filming this!"

Then to Eshan, he said, "I am going to slit your throat and watch you bleed. Then later, Sabia and I are going to watch you die, over and over and over again!"

Just as Musad was about to cut deeply into Eshan's flesh, watched closely by the hired thugs, he was interrupted by a voice coming from just a few steps behind them all.

Appearing from the side of a recycling bin, Zac spoke in a cold, calm, husky voice. "Put the knife down, you really do not want to do that."

Everyone turned at once but were relieved to discover just one brave yet muscular *fool* and a pretty young woman, stood before them.

Eshan was instantly and carelessly dropped to the floor, Musad and his gang were content with the maths and looking forward to teaching this idiot and his girlfriend a brutal lesson they would not forget!

Altogether, the four yobs walked towards Zac, as Musad excitedly prepared himself to watch this free and unexpected piece of entertainment.

"If you turn and leave now, I will not hurt any one of you," Zac stated.

Leah was asking herself, how and why she had involved them in this nightmare? She ran over to Eshan, unnoticed in the evolving drama and used her scarf to wipe away some blood from his eyes.

He groaned, "Help me, please help me. My phone, inside my jacket. Please, please, find my phone."

Eshan leaned over slightly, allowing Leah to locate the phone and give it to him. With shaking hands, he managed to call his friend.

"Rafi... come armed... send someone to Sabia... Musad is back."

Eshan held Leah's hand, "Do not worry, my friends will be here any minute to help us," he assured her.

However, both Eshan and Leah watched, astounded, with mouths wide open, as Zac dealt with each member of the hired help, sending them hurtling through the air and landing painfully onto the ground. They had attacked Zac from every direction, with vicious looking knives, but not once, had any one of them succeeded in getting close enough to even scratch his skin.

When the last of the yobs had sensibly fled for their lives, Zac was about to turn and check on Leah. This was the moment Musad chose to run out from his hiding place behind him, suddenly appearing and thrusting his blade deep into Zac's back with all of his might. Leah was unaware of these events, as she was wiping blood from Eshan's cut hand, however Eshan had witnessed Zac's injury and was now fearing the worst.

The sharp piercing and intense pain in Zac's back was eased as the blade was slowly rejected out of his body, then it dropped down onto the ground below. Zac turned and grabbed Musad by the throat, lifting him high into the air. Without releasing his tight grip, he pressed Musad hard against a brick wall and held him there.

Musad was terrified! He knew he had stabbed his knife through Zac's entire body, yet he was miraculously healing before his very eyes!

Zac put his face closer to Musad's, "Leave Lincoln tonight or I will come for you. I will rip you to pieces. Do you understand?"

Wet cowardly tears fell from Musad's sweaty round face. He was shaking as urine trickled down his stubby legs. Zac threw him onto the wet hard ground. Musad scrambled to his feet. Completely soiled and petrified, he could not turn and run fast enough to escape. It was actually, quite a comical sight to see.

Zac now walked towards Leah, who was assisting Eshan to stand.

"Are you both alright?" he asked them.

Before they had time to answer, a bright yellow Toyota Yaris, sped into the carpark, then screeched to a halt besides them. Rafi, his friend and the driver, Mahdi, jumped out from the front. Two others followed from the backseats.

"Eshan! Are you badly hurt? Where is Musad?" asked Mahdi.

"I am alright, Mahdi, but my concern is for Sabia! Musad is probably on his way to her now!" Eshan replied fearfully.

"Well, I hope he does go to her!" Rafi declared, knowing that Sabia, his sister, was now in safe and protective hands, "I called her friends, Jaz and Shania, straight after your call. They are with her now."

Leah was surprised on hearing her friends' names mentioned and also of Eshan's huge sigh of relief on hearing this news.

Eshan then began to explain, "I would be dead now, if it were not for my new friends here. I..."

In a split of a second, events suddenly, became seriously frightening and dramatic as, without warning, Rafi produced a long dagger while the other three men brandished bows and golden pointed arrowheads which were aimed directly at Zac.

"What are you doing?" Leah yelled, running to Zac's side and taking hold of his hand.

Eshan stepped forward, "No! I owe him my life, Rafi. I cannot allow you to destroy him."

Rafi was fuming, "But ... you know *what* he is?"

"Yes, I do," Eshan acknowledged, "I do not understand why he helped me either, but he did. And the young woman with him, she is *an innocent*."

Leah had had enough, "I cannot believe this! My friend just saved your friend's life! Are you all completely mad?"

Mahdi stepped forward, "Put your weapons down!" he ordered his Warriors, then directed his following words to Zac, "We are grateful that Allah sent you to help our friend today. I suspect that we will all meet again soon. I pray we will still be fighting on the same side."

Mahdi then returned to their car, followed closely by the others. Eshan held back and placed a small card into Leah's hand.

"Here," he whispered, "Call this number if you ever find yourself in a difficult situation and need our help." Then he thoughtfully added, "Be careful, I do not believe you understand who ... or *what* you are involved with."

Leah stood silently beside Zac, pondering Eshan's words, as the two cars exited the carpark.

Meanwhile, having received a *distress call* from Eshan's friend, Rafi, Shania and Jaz had immediately left The Forum and sped to Sabia and Musad's marital home. They had already voiced their concerns to Sadaat, Rafi and Eshan about Sabia's safety since she had taken legal steps to end her marriage. The three men had been devastatingly shocked to discover what kind of a life,

Sabia had been secretly subjected to.

Eshan was especially affected, having known that on the same day Sabia had announced her engagement to Musad, he had been just hours away from confessing his own love to her. He had hated himself for not acting sooner though, to his cost, he was living through the hardest few weeks of his life. Work was crazy and he had begun his secret training with Mahdi. He was not to know that his only true love, was being hastily pursued by Musad, the man whom he had detested upon their first meeting and from then onwards, had deliberately avoided at the Mosque.

Jaz and Shania had arrived speedily at the house and left shortly after, confident that Sabia was safe and well.

Musad had been too traumatised from his experience at the carpark to show up again. He now believed that Sabia was being protected by her family and friends, so he would just have to wait a while before making his next despicable move.

Jaz had first met Sabia, a beautiful and talented former ballet instructor, when Robyn had asked her for her help. Robyn and her police colleagues had been called by neighbours on more than just a few occasions, having heard Musad's rages travel through the open windows of their properties. The officers would be appalled to find Sabia distressed and beaten. Frustratingly, each time she remained too frightened to press charges against her abusive husband.

Robyn feared for the innocent young woman, as the frequency and brutality of the attacks were increasing. She asked Jaz for advice on how she could involve Shania, with her experience of counselling domestic abuse victims, without the knowledge of Musad. That same week, Jaz had contacted Sabia, asking her whether she would be interested in teaching a toddler's ballet class at The Forum. To their relief, Sabia accepted and was overjoyed to be offered the opportunity of leaving the house one afternoon a week, while her husband was away at work. Jaz and

Robyn suspected that she intended to keep these afternoons a secret from him. That suited their purpose well.

This new arrangement was to change Sabia's life forever. Each week, Sabia along with Amir, her constant four-legged companion, were collected from her house by Jaz and taken to The Forum. Once there, she had the pleasure of teaching a thirty-minute ballet class to a group of five adorable toddlers. Zoe was more than happy to take care of Amir. Jaz taught a two-hour class in another room, leaving an hour and a half for Sabia to sit waiting for her, while enjoying a coffee with her *new friend*, Shania.

Sabia found Shania's work as a counsellor, fascinating. Their frank and honest discussions plus Shania's professional and personal skills, enabled Sabia to understand the reasons for and behind, her undeserving abuse. Sabia learned about *gas-lighting* and that her suffering had been due to Musad's inadequacies, not her own. Indeed, her beauty, talents, achievements and desirability, only magnified his own shortfalls, failings and incompetence, adding fuel to the burning fire of his jealousy.

As the facts became clearer in her mind, Sabia's thoughts were no longer clouded. She realised Musad had crept into her life when she was vulnerable. Her brother's friend, the only man she knew she could ever really love, Eshan, had spurned her affections. It had taken all her courage on that memorable day, to finally tell him how she had felt about him since their first meeting.

Eshan had come to Lincoln to train as a doctor at the hospital where Rafi, her brother, also worked. They had become instant friends and Eshan was a regular dinner guest at their house. She had been sure that he had feelings for her too, so often their eyes met, and moments spent with him always felt so special.

At a party, to celebrate her nineteenth birthday and for receiving the final certificate, awarding her the status of a Qualified Instructor of Ballet, her family and friends gathered in the family's garden. She had spent her entire young life studying hard at school while painfully enduring hours of training, dancing and assisting with the teaching of classes, at her beloved dance school. She believed that this, her birthday, would be the day she told Eshan, everything.

Sabia was not to know that the decision she had made, could not have been implemented on a worse day.

Eshan's Story

Eshan was a remarkable young doctor at the University Hospital, Lincoln. He had known from a young age what was expected of him; to be a good Muslim, an obedient son, a patient and loving older brother to his five younger siblings, a diligent student and to one day, become a fine Doctor of Medicine.

Life had not been easy for Eshan. Memories of his childhood were not particularly happy ones, there were never enough hours in the day to fulfil his daily duties of schooling and the numerous household chores. He awoke early and found sleep difficult while sharing a bedroom with two of his younger brothers.

Eshan enjoyed his school-life; he found the lessons interesting and learning came easy to him. There, he was free to play and to make mistakes. He was popular with his peers and teachers, being an intelligent and talented student in the classroom, as well as outside on the sports field. While constantly remaining humble and a good friend to all, he was gracious and had a strong sense of justice, wanting to speak up for those less fluent, or able, than himself.

Adding to his attributes, Eshan was blessed with perfect brown skin, dark smouldering eyes and a smile that melted many hearts as he grew into manhood.

When Eshan had first arrived in Lincoln, ready to begin his new position at the hospital, he had been slightly dubious at the prospect of living with his quiet grandmother Dharma and strict grandfather, Zeeshan. It was, however, an enlightening experience becoming greater acquainted with his elderly grandparents.

Eshan had once considered Dharma serene and submissive while Zeeshan was stern and serious. How wrong he had been! He witnessed first-hand, their day to day routine of deep love and respect for one another. His grandfather had extensive knowledge of religion and history while Dharma had amazing problem-solving skills and a deeper common sense. Eshan soon decided that she should be running the country, not the Prime Minister!

The things Eshan loved the most about his grandparents were their humour; how they were always laughing, even when their favourite television programme did not seem overly hilarious to him, they would find it so. And Dharma always called his grandfather *ZeeZee* when at home, and he called her *Dharma-Darling*. Never would they leave the house together without holding hands. Eshan enjoyed many long discussions with them both and listened to their wise words of knowledge and experience about life, work, marriage and people.

Life had become so much better for Eshan having moved to a beautiful city, also living with his grandparents provided him with the added luxury of his own quiet bedroom. He had a good friend in Rafi, who like himself, enjoyed debating anything from the world economy to conspiracy theories about Covid 19 and different interpretations of religious texts. Although, not always in agreement, the two young men respected one another's opinions.

Rafi often invited Eshan back to his beautiful family home. Rafi's father Sadaat and his mother, Safie, made him a welcome and frequent visitor.

Rafi had introduced Eshan to Sabia, his younger sister, on his first visit and he had immediately recognised *the most exquisite girl he had ever seen*, from their Mosque. She was intelligent, funny and ambitious and he loved the moments when she would remain, after dinner, and be part of his and Rafi's conversations.

Eshan had been invited to celebrate Sabia's birthday and was surprised to receive a text from Rafi in the early hours of that morning, asking him to come to the house immediately.

He was exhausted from having worked an extra-long shift which had been challenging and distressing; one of Eshan's patients had been a young pregnant drug-addict. He had fought hard to save her baby but was forced to later explain to the mother and her intoxicated boyfriend, that the new precious life they had created together, had not survived. The boyfriend had begun shouting, calling Eshan racist names. The young woman became hysterical, screaming blame at her boyfriend for having pushed her down some steps earlier that day. Security had been called; Eshan, two nurses and a security guard were all hurt while restraining the couple. A few hours later, the woman insisted on leaving the hospital with her boyfriend, no doubt going in search of their next fix.

On nightshifts like this, Eshan hated his job, he hated people. Now, having just rested his weary head on the soft soothing pillow, Eshan then received Rafi's text.

Driving along the dark, quiet streets, Eshan thought of Sabia and how he would love to have a family with her someday. He would be a tolerant father, allowing and encouraging his children to choose their own paths in life, unlike his own. And Sabia would be a wonderful mother. *Maybe his children would be born with her dancing talents?*

As Eshan pulled into the large driveway, he was surprised to see Rafi and Sadaat already waiting for him in a yellow Toyota Yaris, belonging to a young man he recognised from their Mosque, called Mahdi.

The door was opened and Eshan joined Rafi in the back seat. A short drive later, the car pulled on to the driveway of an old detached house, sat on a hill. The mansion, though old, was well-kept and surrounded by large beautiful gardens, where more cars were parked, secluded by the thick hedges and ancient trees.

The men got out of the car and Eshan followed silently behind as they entered the house. He noticed colourful writing and different symbols painted creatively around the columns inside the entrance hall. A huge wooden door was unlocked and Eshan found himself standing in a magnificent room where he noted a painting on the wall of Saladin; the victorious General who in 1187, opposed the Crusaders at Hattin. On another wall hung a painting of Nasir al-Din al-Tusi's observatory in Maragha, Iran which is recognised as the most advanced in the Islamic world during the 13th Century. It depicted the early star gazers and mathematicians busy at their work.

Other religious artwork and unique ornaments upon opulent pieces of furniture filled and decorated every space of the room, including a 16th Century Iznik plate depicting a Mediterranean ship on rough dangerous seas, placed on an intricately carved wooden table standing beside an ancient looking wooden door. The words Bayt al-Hikma; 'House of Wisdom' were carved into the wood. Mahdi opened it and the three men stood back allowing Eshan to enter the next room first.

Eshan found himself stood before an audience of around twenty men and women, some of whom he recognised from his Mosque. He could not believe his tired and swollen eyes, for this room completely took his breath away.

The ceilings and walls were decorated with vibrantly coloured waves of silk, swirling and shimmering in the bright lights flowing from the golden elaborate wall-lamps. The wooden floor had thick luxurious rugs, of different styles and colours, from all over the world.

His silent audience were sensibly spaced out and seated at small wooden polished tables, positioned all around the room. Cushions of every size, colour and fabric, were scattered about. Each table was set with golden goblets and small golden jewelled-edged plates offering delicious dried fruits, nuts, dates and other tempting delicacies.

The group of faces sat silently as Eshan stood before them. Mahdi and Sadaat each joined tables that had a place setting already prepared for them.

Rafi began to introduce Eshan to their attentive audience, explaining his background and achievements. He then began to introduce the men and women to Eshan, giving brief accounts of their various professions.

As Rafi had finished speaking, a door hidden from view by a column of bright orange silk, which was hanging from the ceiling to the ground, suddenly opened. A group of four young men and two women appeared and all smiled and acknowledged him. Eshan was introduced to each individual and then Mahdi stood.

"We all want to welcome you, Eshan," he said, "It is your destiny to become one of us. If you agree, you are to train as a Warrior; a Protector of the Good and to be part of an ever-growing resistance against *Evil*. Will you join us Eshan?"

"Yes. I am honoured," came the reply.

Mahdi continued, "You will now learn more of our secrets, but first you are required to perform an Oath of Silence. You can never divulge anything that we reveal to you from this day forward. Do you understand?"

"Yes, I do," Eshan replied.

Eshan was led into the long room behind the orange veil. This space was void and empty, except for the various weapons that hung upon the stone walls of the ancient and original part of the house.

Eshan performed the Oath witnessed by Mahdi, Rafi and the six other Warriors. He swore that everything he was to be taught, from that day onwards about religion, history and their modern-day relevance, would never be revealed or discussed outside of these walls. He also took an Oath never to divulge secrets from his future classes of Vira Vidya, the Science of a Warrior and Yuddha-vidya, their secret Combat Knowledge.

Eshan arrived home during the late morning. He collapsed onto his bed and slept soundly for the next few hours. On waking, he quickly showered and changed into his casual but smart black trousers and a sky-blue silk shirt. The late afternoon sun was still shining, and his tired head ached. Countless revelations: some marvellous and inspiring, while others were terrifying, each one, painfully swirling around inside his overworked brain.

By the time Eshan arrived at Sabia's birthday party, he was feeling awful; every single sound seemed to vibrate, causing his head more pain. His eyes were swollen and sore.

Sabia had led him straight into the garden, where there was a large gazebo containing small groups of tables and chairs with colourful displays of delicious food and drink. Eshan was greeted by lots of faces he already knew and a couple he recognised from having met just a few short hours before.

It was a little later, when the background music had become slower and most of the other guests had left, that Sabia asked Eshan to dance with her. This was the moment she had chosen to reveal her undying love. However, Eshan did not respond in the way she had expected him to. He hardly said anything at all. After the song had finished playing, Eshan had kissed her hand and then left her party.

The following few weeks, Eshan's life was spent working at the hospital or training with Mahdi, Rafi and the other secret Warriors. Sabia, in the meantime, hurt and humiliated having felt rejected by the man she loved, was left vulnerable and exposed to the scheming advances of Musad.

Sabia's Story

Musad had wanted Sabia since first setting eyes on her at the Mosque. He had recently sold his mortgaged flat in London and was now able to pay in full, the much lower price for his modern four bedroomed house, on a smart new estate by a river, in Lincoln. He was a Manager for a large supermarket chain, which made his relocation simple.

To Sabia, Musad was a charming, successful date, who took her to lovely restaurants and treated her respectfully whenever they spent time together in his stylish home. When he had surprised her with a marriage proposal, after just a month of dating, she was as surprised as her family were, when she accepted. Musad insisted on arranging it for the following month, no expense spared and Sabia was made to feel like a princess on her big day.

At the Wedding Celebration, Sabia was even presented with a beautiful black fluffy Shepadoodle puppy (an Alsatian crossed with a large Poodle) with huge paws and complete with a big red bow around his neck. The guests had loved this gesture; however, it had left Eshan feeling sick to his stomach.

Although she knew she did not love Musad, or indeed, find him attractive, Sabia had decided that loving someone was too painful and that this was an opportunity for her to have a good life with a kind and successful man who appeared to love her. Afterall, she had the career she had worked so hard for: teaching ballet at the School of Dance she herself, had been a pupil since the age of three. She had been sure that her life could still be a happy one. Never would she have imagined that Musad was in truth, a jealous controlling bully. The cruel manipulation and violent treatment of her husband would be revealed just one week into their marriage.

One of the many ways Musad chose to punish his gentle young

wife was by threatening to sell, hurt or kill her most cherished possession, the puppy he had already named, Amir. As the torment escalated over the following weeks and months, Sabia was manipulated into leaving her job and rarely attended the Mosque, deciding it would be better to concentrate on keeping the house and garden just how Musad wanted it.

Musad did not like Sabia working, seeing other people or having her own money and finally had her believing that her family and friends would now consider her an embarrassment. This could not have been further from the truth; her parents Sadaat and Safie, her brother Rafi, and Eshan had all suffered sleepless nights worrying that she had chosen to suddenly distance herself from everyone. They could not understand her recent extreme weight-loss and her fragile and hostile mental state.

In a short time, Sabia had lost her self-confidence and the ability to think rationally for herself. Her only joy was her darling, Amir; the terrified young dog who hid shaking, behind a sofa every time he heard his master come home. Luckily, Musad was out of the house most of the time, working long and unsociable hours, or meeting up with his despicable friend, Mike.

Sabia and Amir found love and companionship in one another. As Amir grew into a fine strong handsome dog, so grew Musad's threats of teaching his *useless wife* a lesson by selling Amir to Mike. Sabia did all she could to keep Amir out of their sight and had trained the young dog well; Amir obediently remained silent, crouched behind the sofa, even during the worst of her beatings.

On many occasions, the couple living next door had called the police but Musad would always leave the house immediately on hearing the siren, feeling confident Sabia would not dare press any legal charges against him.

Robyn's colleagues would usually find Amir shaking, whimpering, as he lay faithfully beside his mistress. Robyn had decided to attend the calls herself, as they became more frequent and violent. Turning to Jaz for a way to help this young victim, was to change Sabia's destiny.

Following her last life-threatening attack, Musad was forced to leave their home and he subsequently moved in with his like-minded friend, Mike.

Once recovered, Sabia began taking private lessons from Jaz at The Forum. Her ballet training had created a muscular body, perfect for the combat skills Jaz could teach her. In fact, Sabia persistently astounded Jaz, with the speed in which she could learn and without doubt, became her most talented pupil, *ever*.

Meanwhile, Amir was also evolving, constantly impressing Sabia with his intelligence and other *gifts*, secretly bestowed upon him by Zoe. Mistress and canine now shared a *special* and spiritual connection.

RIVALS

As Zac drove his car into the carpark and pulled up in-front of the entrance to The Forum, Leah immediately felt guilty as Shania, Mac and Taylor came running down the steps to greet them. Their faces revealed the worry caused by Leah's thoughtlessness in not informing them of her change of plans. For they had been expecting her to attend the Sunday Service and had been horrified to watch her leave The Forum and enter Zac's car on the screens of their watch-devices.

Taylor had provided all the knights with the best technology, allowing them to instantly observe from any of the cameras placed outside The Forum, Howard and Zoe's home and various other important premises.

"Where have you been? I have been so worried about you. Why didn't you answer your phone?" Shania asked, holding open the passenger door of the Range Rover.

Leah felt awful, she had not once checked her phone or even considered informing her friends throughout the day about her whereabouts.

"I am so sorry," she replied. "We went for a coffee, then some-one needed our help. We got mixed up in an awful incident and I lost track of time."

Zac was stood in front of his car, staring into the stern faces of Taylor and Mac.

"This was all my fault. I apologise," he said coldly.

Taylor replied, "We know."

The two men glared at one another as Shania began to lead Leah towards the entrance of The Forum. Mac turned and followed them inside.

"Do you have something you wish to say to me?" Zac asked Taylor.

"I want you to stay away from Leah," Taylor firmly replied.

Zac sniggered, "Am I supposed to care about what you want?"

Zac was feeling a mixture of emotions; he was angry but not because he was being challenged. The truth of the matter was that he suspected this young man of having feelings for Leah and this enraged him. He was surprised at his own jealousy and of the conflicting deliberations he was suddenly experiencing.

Taylor spoke again, "I am warning you! Do not see her, speak to her, or even think of her ever again!"

"Oh, I see now," Zac mocked, "You are worried in case I steal your girl away from you, aren't you *Bible Boy*? What's the matter; frightened she isn't as wholesome and innocent as you thought?"

His vile words were inflicted upon Taylor to create offence and fury, and they worked.

Engulfed with manic rage, Taylor threw himself at Zac like a violent strike of lightening. Using speed and skill, Taylor had Zac pinned down on the ground, face down. Taylor then produced a small golden weapon with a jewelled handle and held the blade to Zac's face.

Zac made the decision not to retaliate; he could hear Taylor's heavy breathing and had recognised his combat skills as those taught to the old *Knights of Temple Breuer*. *His weapon could pos-*

sibly be one of the lost artifacts.

Suddenly, Zac felt Taylor roughly pulled off of him and he immediately stood, just in time to see Mac grab the weapon from Taylor's hand and conceal it within his jacket. Zac recognised it at once – he had seen the craftmanship before, however, not in *this* Century.

Mac and Stephen were stood either side of Taylor.

"What do you think you are doing?" Stephen demanded of Taylor.

Mac now addressed Zac, "We apologise for our friend's behaviour. Can't imagine what must have provoked him," he said sarcastically, then continued, "It would be better ... safer, if you never returned here again."

Zac said nothing, as Mac and Stephen escorted Taylor, seething with frustration, back inside of The Forum.

A few seconds after climbing into the driver's seat of his car and starting the ignition, Zac noticed Raama suddenly appear across the road from the carpark, in front of the fields. Zac collected him and they drove away together.

"So, what have you learned?" Raama asked.

Zac considered his reply for a moment, "There are young people displaying the secret teachings of combat, once used by the old Knights of Temple Bruer. They must be the ones who eliminated your *brother* for they have somehow managed to obtain sacred weapons. And today, I also met a group of *interesting* Muslims, they knew *what* I was."

Raama appeared, confused, "*They* have obtained *old knowledge* too?"

"Yes," replied Zac, "And they have also acquired *distinct armaments.*"

Raama thought for a moment, then, "What about the girl? Is she a threat?"

"No!" Zac replied, too quickly. Realising his mistake and quickly recovering, "She is just a singer in the band, but she has close friendships with those who might be. I will keep close to her; win her trust and I will get the information we need."

"Good!" Raama said, cheerfully, "Find out their plans and where they are getting their information and weapons from. This could be the most dangerous threat to our master yet, do you understand?"

Zac thought for a moment, "Yes," he said, "I think I do. I will meet the girl again tomorrow, get her away from her protective friends and learn what I can."

Monday

Shania had already left their apartment earlier for work and Leah was preparing herself for a day of study. She would complete another piece of her coursework, then go out for some cool fresh air and treat herself to a coffee by The Brayford.

Later that morning, while sitting, enjoying her surroundings and the taste of her milky coffee, Leah felt her soul rejoice on suddenly hearing Zac's unexpected voice.

"Hi," he said, "How are you today?" Then he sat himself down on the wall beside her.

"I am good, thank you. What are you doing here?" she enquired.

"Enjoying some fresh air. Fancy a walk?" he asked her.

Leah smiled and threw away her empty cup in a nearby bin, before they walked side by side, along the pavement leading to the City Centre. When they crossed a busy road, Zac protectively took hold of Leah's hand then didn't let go of it again. Leah did not mind.

Later, as the couple began walking up Steep Hill, towards the Castle and Cathedral, they passed Mac's shop. Leah looked inside and was relieved to see Mac busy discussing an antique clock with a customer, at the far end of the premises.

Minutes later, they passed a building which sent a shock through Zac's soul. He suddenly remembered that gruesome night in the freezing January of 1289. He and Raama were amongst the Jewish Community which had settled in Lincoln. They were good, honest, hard-working people, enjoying a time of growth and prosperity for which they deserved.

Raama had found it easy to enlist a few jealous locals, who were happy to start trouble, assisting him in his plan to murder a respected young rabbi, Jacob, and his family.

As the fires broke out and the rioting began, Zac remembered how Raama had hunted Jacob's wife and her two children as they were fleeing down the hill. Her attempt to hide behind a large ancient ritual stone was thwarted by the cries of her youngest terrified child. On discovering them, Raama callously murdered each one.

Zachariah had been instructed to kill the rabbi who was inside the small synagogue. When Zachariah found him, dressed completely in black and wearing his long black hair beneath a turban, Jacob was attempting to conceal a small child under a blanket, in the far corner of the room.

Jacob looked up to discover Zachariah stood behind him and his face filled with horror. Zachariah lifted the blanket with the tip of his sword, to discover the tear-stained face of a frightened and trembling child, of no more than eight years old.

"Please," Jacob had begged, "Not the child!"

Zachariah had known that he could not help Jacob, however, the child brought back memories, those of his village and of his own parents. He decided he *could* give Jacob a precious gift, a small personal sentimental *token* for the loss of his own father, Ananias. He knew he had to act swiftly and without hesitation, so he grabbed the child and carried him over to a window which, the room being below ground level, opened onto the street. The boy managed to crawl through the small opening, then once outside, began to sob.

"Everyone is fighting, Papa!" he called back through the window.

"Tell him to run," Zachariah instructed Jacob sternly.

Zachariah watched Jacob take something out of his tunic pocket and then grab hold of his son's trembling hand above him. He placed a small brown leather pouch into it. Jacob instructed his young terrified son.

"Go straight to the Cathedral, the way your mother showed you. Bishop Hugh will take care of you. Give him this pouch and tell him these words, *'David's Stone is for the Jew to use, when the time comes.'* Now, go!"

Feeling Raama in the close vicinity, Zachariah moved quickly and called to Jacob, "Rabbi! Come over here, away from the window!"

Jacob immediately obeyed and saw Raama enter the room. He bravely stood before Zachariah and looking into the cold dark eyes, whispered, "Thank you."

The sword was swiftly and deeply thrust into Jacob's body. It slumped but remained upright, supported for just a few seconds by the rigid metal sword inside of it. As Zachariah withdrew the long blade, Jacob grabbed hold of his muscular forearm, squeezing it tightly, before falling to the ground.

Once more, he whispered, "You will be forgiven."

Raama smiled and was satisfied with what he had just seen. He had not heard Jacob's dying words, but Zachariah had, and he would always remember them.

"Zac! Are you okay?" asked Leah, again. "Earth to Zac, come in, are you reading?" Grateful to be released from the memory, he smiled.

"Sorry," he said, "My mind wandered."

Leah was still a little out of breath when they reached the top of Steep Hill. They walked around the Cathedral Quarter before finding a small café with an outside dining area. They sat down and were immediately greeted by a pretty female waitress. She took their orders of two white coffees and cheese and tomato toasted sandwiches, and shortly returned with it. Her flirtatious smiles were wasted on Zac, as he sipped his hot coffee and stared only into Leah's eyes.

Zac found Leah fascinating and could not understand how or why, she had drawn him to her, from that very first moment. There was an undeniable and unexplainable connection. She had seemed to him at first to be fragile and innocent, however, when she had led him to the rescuing of the young Muslim, some sort of power, that even she did not understand herself, had mysteriously come over her.

Leah found herself studying Zac's dark eyes and *felt* his painful past and a complicated present. She had never experienced such a strong desire to be with a person in her whole life until now, it was like a mystical magnetic force pulling their two souls together.

Could this be love? She instantly chastened her wandering thoughts; *you hardly even know this man!*

Suddenly, Zac asked, "Leah, could you trust me?"

"What a strange question," Leah stated. "Do I have a reason, not to trust you?"

"Oh, my beautiful, wonderful Leah. What are you doing to me?" Zac sighed.

Leah smiled, "I have never felt like I am feeling right now, with anybody. I have never met anyone like you before."

Zac replied, "No, thankfully, you probably haven't." They both smiled, continuing to search the other's eyes for some kind of answers to their own, many, unspoken questions.

"How well do you know Howard?" Zac asked.

"Not terribly well but I instantly liked him when I first met him," she replied, then continued, "What he has achieved with The Forum is incredible. He has a whole community, supporting ... teaching ... feeding ... caring for, one another. It doesn't matter what religion, what background you are from, he just cares about *people* and about our world and its future. Isn't that wonderful?"

There was a moment of silence.

Then, "I don't think you belong at The Forum, Leah," Zac continued meaningfully, "As Howard and your friends become more ... well known ... stronger, then so will the opposition. You could be in a lot of danger."

Leah was mortified, "What? How can you say that?" she continued passionately, "Of course good people, good things, will always face opposition! There are some awful people out there, doing awful things! But we can choose to focus on the positives and support those who are trying their best to make this world a better one. Just because the idiotic hypocrites, the wicked and the greedy seem to always have the loudest voices, does not mean that we have to listen to them! We can act on those *quieter, less popular* but *virtuous* desires of our hearts. We all have a choice, Zac."

Silence, once more ensued. Both sipped their coffee and finished their lunches. Then Zac stood and handed the attentive young waitress a piece of paper currency and told her to keep the change. She was happily astounded at the amount.

Leah followed Zac across the cobbled area leading towards the front of the mighty Cathedral and together they stood under an archway, staring up at the magnificent monument before them.

"Breathtakingly beautiful, isn't it?" Leah said.

Zac's mind was in torment, he hated his existence. He hated *who* and *what*, he was. *Surely he deserved a few precious, moments of joy, happiness and privacy?* He knew Raama would not be able

127

to enter these *sacred walls*.

His battling mind was settled, "Let's go inside," he said.

Taking hold of Leah's hand, Zac led her through the entrance, blending in with the other tourists. He bought their tickets and led her past the Morning Chapel, Ringer's Chapel and the giftshop. A few people were already sat praying in the Nave.

They took interest in the *12ᵗʰ Century Font* and the *carvings by William Fairbank*, of Christ's journey to the Cross and of his Resurrection. Standing in the area of *The Crossing*, where the North and South Transepts met, on the right, they marvelled at the magnificent Great Rose Window, containing fragments of medieval glass, known as *The Bishop's Eye*.

To their left, was *The Dean's Eye Window*. Zac explained to Leah that it had been first installed around the 1200s and tells of the Last Judgment.

"It faces North," he said, "Where Evil was believed to come from."

Zac continued walking until he came to The *Choir Screen*, built in the 1330s to separate the choir, clergy and their assistants from the congregation who stood in the Nave. He hesitated beneath the 4,000 pipes of the 1898 Willis Organ then led Leah into one of the oldest parts of the building known as *St Hugh's Choir*. She couldn't stop herself from touching the wings of the great brass eagle, *The Lectern*, holding a Bible, which stood upon a globe, symbolising the Word of God being carried throughout the world.

Zac watched the joy suddenly drain from her face, "What's the matter? Are you okay?" he asked.

"I am sure many good people have stood within these walls, however, there have been many, many wicked souls too," she replied.

"What makes you say that Leah?"

"I can *feel* it," she said.

"How do you *feel* about me? Do I have a good or a wicked soul?" Zac inquired of her.

Zac held both her hands now and they gazed into one another's eyes. Leah said nothing. Zac brought her hands to his mouth and then kissed them.

A group of Italian tourists suddenly entered this *small church within the Church,* so Zac led Leah out into the space leading to the South East Transept. A large display board stood in the far corner, in front of an ancient thick curtain.

Leah watched Zac move the board forward a little, then disappear behind the curtain. Seconds later, he reappeared and called to her. He had opened an old wooden door and she hesitantly followed him into a small private chapel. It was stone walled all around, void, with no windows just gaps in one of the walls, allowing in small rays of light. Leah shivered with cold.

"Are we allowed in here?" she asked him anxiously.

"No," he replied, "Probably not," and walked over to a small age-old oak table holding two 12th Century Italian bronze candlesticks. It was the only piece of furniture in there. He took a small box of matches from his pocket and lit the old candles. The golden flames danced on the stones of the chapel walls, creating a warm glow and a surreal atmosphere.

To Leah and Zac, it felt like the rest of the world, the universe, did not exist.

Zac took Leah's hand and kissed it. The feel of his soft warm lips ignited a burning fire inside of her and she longed to feel their fullness upon her own. He used his free arm to pull her closer until she felt his muscular chest pressing firmly against her own aching body. She moved her other hand, greedily exploring his broad shoulder beneath the leather jacket, the back of his neck and his thick soft hair. Lowering his head now, releasing her hand, they were both free to wrap their arms around one another.

Their kiss was slow and gentle at first, but their passion and need intensified until Zac, using every last piece of his inner strength to end the ecstatic feeling, pulled away.

"We should go," he said, huskily.

Leaving the Cathedral, Zac and Leah walked outside into the chilly and damp late afternoon air. Holding hands, they quietly and slowly made their way back into the City Centre by a different route.

Stood beneath the *Arch of The Guildhall*, Leah was disappointed when Zac suddenly stood her at arms-length.

"I must leave you here," he said. "Go straight home, won't you?"

"Oh, okay. Yes, of course," Leah was confused, *had she said or done something wrong?*

She began to head for home, feeling emotionally exhausted.

"Take care Leah," Zac whispered before turning and immediately walking into the same direction from which he had seen Raama appear moments earlier.

Once met up with Raama, Zac continued walking in the direction leading away from the City Centre, Raama followed his lead.

"So, what is happening? Is she still useful to us?" Raama asked, impatiently.

"Like I said before, she's just a singer. I won't waste my time on her again," Zac said, secretly dying inside.

"It doesn't matter, anyway," Raama began, "I have called upon my Brothers and Sisters. This is all getting out of control here and The Forum, its Leader and these *blasted New Age Knights* must be destroyed. It will be difficult enough to wipe out the legacy, as it is! Luckily, there are always those few pathetic, weak and jealous mortals who are yearning to tell a few lies, cause some trouble. I will let them loose once the place has been obliterated."

Zac withheld his true emotions well. For he had already decided, earlier that day, inside the secret Chapel within the Cathedral, that he was prepared to protect Leah, at any cost. His own existence had now become irrelevant, only hers mattered.

"When do we make our move?" Zac asked.

"The remaining few of the *others*, will be arriving tonight," Raama revealed, "Either tomorrow, or possibly, the day after, so I will be contacting you again soon. Be ready!"

"That's good," Zac lied, "I will be."

The two men parted and went their separate ways.

Meanwhile, it had occurred to Leah that she didn't even have a means of contacting Zac. She wondered whether she should run back after him, turning around just in time to see him disappear down a side road with another man. She recognised the man immediately. Suddenly, fear and doubt overwhelmed her.

She needed to get home, she felt weak and dizzy.

Leah considered, for a moment, calling Shania. She was unsure whether she was well enough to make it home by herself. However, she remembered that Shania was already doing some counselling sessions at The Forum this afternoon and had planned to stay there for her training session with Jaz, later tonight.

With difficulty, Leah eventually made it home. She dropped heavily and painfully onto her bed, as the fever overwhelmed her.

Minutes later, Zac arrived outside her apartment. He was deeply concerned on discovering the door slightly ajar. Warily, he stepped inside into the lounge area. Suddenly, he could hear her. Leah's whimpering and suffering could be overheard coming from another room.

Opening the door, Zac found Leah, unconscious, lying on the

bed, in a fever and sweating profusely. He ran over to her and swept her up into his strong and tender arms, then took her into the lounge and placed her gently onto the sofa. Next, he rushed to the bathroom and held a small hand towel under the cold tap, then wrung it before using it to wipe Leah's burning face and neck.

Just then, Zac was alerted to Leah's mobile phone, buzzing from inside her bag, which was lying on the floor by the entrance door. He decided to check it, it might be one of her friends calling.

He needed to speak with them somehow.

The call identification said, 'Shania'. Suddenly, without the need to unlock, or answer the call, Shania's face appeared on the screen.

"We know you are with Leah," she said, having been alerted by her device that their apartment had been entered by a stranger. Zac's picture had sent a jolt of fear throughout her, "Do her any harm and we will destroy you before this day ends."

"She has a bad fever!" Zac said into the phone, ignoring the threats, "I don't know how to help her!"

There was a quiet thoughtful moment before, "Keep her calm, cool her temperature and she will come out of it on her own in just a few minutes," Shania instructed calmly.

"It's urgent that I speak to you and your friends tonight," Zac said, "I must warn Howard and it's vital that you trust me."

Leah's fever was cooling down. She was now awake and wearily opening her eyes.

"Are you able to bring Leah to The Forum now?" Shania asked him.

"Yes, my car is parked downstairs," Zac replied.

"Yes, we know it is," Shania replied coldly, and then she ended the call.

Zac spent the following few minutes fetching Leah a drink of cold water and explaining to her that he was now going to take her to The Forum. She was confused but compliant. He was bewildered how she could not remember being so ill, just a few minutes previously.

Zac waited while Leah quickly showered and changed into fresh jeans and a warm jumper. Grabbing her warmest coat from its peg, along with her scarf and gloves, Leah then locked her apartment door before following Zac out of the building.

Their journey to The Forum was quiet as neither spoke. Leah's head ached and Zac was anxious, aware he would be entering dangerous and hostile ground.

Meanwhile, The Forum was being vacated, an excuse about the testing of the Air Purifier was enough to quickly empty the building.

Moments before Leah and Zac's arrival, Sabia had appeared coming down the stairs with her loyal Amir by her side, closely followed by Jaz. Both were dressed in their combat training clothes having just finished another intense training session together. Howard instantly informed them of the recent and rapidly developing events.

"If it is okay with everyone, I would like to stay and add my support," Sabia had requested.

Jaz had added, "She is well trained now. I am happy for her to stay if you are, Howard?"

Howard had smiled kindly at Sabia, as if she were a sweet child offering to wash his car for free and not the terrifyingly skilled warrior she had become. For Sabia was now well enough prepared to fight against demons, and brave enough to put herself forward, knowing that she could possibly die for Howard and his cause.

"That would be great," he said.

Sabia spoke a few words to Amir, who then walked over to Zoe and sat obediently by her side. Zoe smiled at Sabia and stroked Amir's head affectionately.

It was becoming dark as Zac and Leah's expected arrival was watched apprehensively by Howard, Zoe, Sabia and the knights, from the security camera screen, inside the foyer of The Forum. The knights had changed into their combat life-saving *armour of mystical cloth*. Sabia had been gifted the same to wear.

As Leah and Zac approached the steps leading up to the opened entrance, the knights took their places.

This was to be the beginning of an exceptionally long night indeed.

ANCESTORS

L eah slowly walked towards the door of The Forum. Zac gently brushed passed her, entering first. She grabbed hold of his hand as they moved through to the silent dining area together.

"Hello!" she called, "Is anyone here?"

At that moment, Leah felt a shocking pain in her arm as Shania had, swiftly and abruptly, grabbed it and torn her away from Zac. Now they had been separated, the knights did not have to fear hurting their friend in the imminent struggle ahead.

Shania held on to Leah's hand assuring her, "It's okay, Leah. Stay here with me, let Howard and the others deal with this." Leah was frightened and confused, but she trusted her dearest friend.

Without any retaliation, Zac had been pounced upon and was now lying on the floor face down, with once again, Taylor holding a knife to his face.

"I am getting really tired of this, *Bible Boy!*" Zac muttered.

Then, quicker than an eye could see, Zac had somehow managed to roll over onto his back, manhandle Taylor and then bring them both to a standing position. However, now, Zac was holding Taylor's knife.

Leah watched in disbelief; her friends and a girl she knew vaguely as one of Jaz's private students, Sabia, were stood united; hostile and prepared for a fight. She noted they were dressed in clothes made from the fabric she immediately recognised. Their military uniforms, revealing each strong, toned and expertly trained body, were made from the same astonishing cloth of that, which she had not long ago discovered lying at the bottom of Shania's training bag.

As Zac held on to Taylor's knife, the two men glared into one another's eyes. Meanwhile, Sabia and the other knights, circled around them. However, unexpectedly, Zac calmly returned the weapon by its blade, allowing Taylor to easily take hold of it by the handle.

"I mean none of you any harm," Zac began, "I need to warn your pastor, Howard, that The Forum will be attacked, possibly as soon as tomorrow."

Stephen now demanded, "By how many? Mortals or *your own kind*?"

Zac replied coldly, "There will be many. Hundreds possibly. There will be an army of a few mortals, but most will be of *my master's kind*. You will need every soul, *sacred weapon* and strategy you have available, to survive this attack. It is designed to wipe you and this place, off the surface of the Earth forever. Your walls will not be strong enough to save you; they will keep your enemy outside, but you will never be able to eliminate their souls permanently. You will fire at them, they will fall, but then they will keep coming back until they have worn you down and killed every single living soul inside." Then he reflected, "Howard should have built his new Temple on the *hallowed soil* of Bruer."

Stepping out from the shadows and shielded by a barrier of his own young protectors, Howard slowly walked towards them all. Zoe and Amir were just a few steps behind him.

Howard stopped, then spoke in a calm, confident tone of authority, "I wanted to build it there originally Zac, but had to be consoled with the open space here and do the best I could with some *sacred* and *protective stones* instead. I have lived in faith that I would eventually discover a way to *cleanse* the land before *this war* began. I had hoped I had more time."

All heads turned to look at Howard as he continued.

"You and your *brother* Raama, came here intending to destroy us. What has changed, I wonder? We must now decide whether you have actually come here tonight to either help us, or to discover where we keep our *secret and sacred weapons*, capable of destroying you and your *friends*."

Zac was amazed and wondered how Howard already knew so much.

Howard continued, "Yes, we were expecting your imminent arrival. You look surprised. What I don't understand though, Zachariah, is how you were able to enter inside our protective walls?"

Leah looked to Shania, "What are they talking about? What does it all mean?" Shania stood quietly and did not answer her troubled friend.

Zac answered the question, "It's simple; I was of mortal birth."

Howards brain, along with the others, were making vital and unbelievable connections.

"Ah! The boy!" he said, "The dark-eyed boy in the village that was burnt to the ground ... the young soldier!"

Zac's face could not hide his astonishment! "How do you know all of this?"

Taylor interrupted, "We will ask the questions, not you!"

Howard looked at his nephew kindly, "It's alright, Taylor." Then he returned his attention to Zac, "Leah told us."

Zac immediately turned and looked directly at her. Leah had never felt so shocked, scared and betrayed in her entire life.

"No, I didn't!" she shouted, "I don't even know what you are all talking about!"

Zoe could take no more, watching the torment Leah was now suddenly exposed to, was too much for her to bare, "Stop! Please, Howard, just stop!"

Everyone darted their attention to the woman whom they had all come to know, love and respect, as Howard's elegant, supportive and unassuming wife.

Zoe walked over to where Leah and Shania were standing, Amir by her side. She then addressed Leah in the kindest manner in which she had shown since first seeing her again, after so many years.

"It is time you knew the truth, Leah." Then speaking to the others, she said, "It is time everyone knew the truth. I believe Leah's destiny has brought her here to us; she has been sent to help us for a purpose."

Leah was becoming more distraught by the second, "What? How am I supposed to help; sing you all a bloody song?"

Shania could see her friend becoming hysterical, "Calm down, it will be okay," she smiled, assuring her softly.

Howard's attention had instantly withdrawn from Zac and was now focused on his spouse, "What do you mean, Zoe? Darling, you need to explain further."

Zoe began, "Leah's birth mother, my dear friend Rose, was born, like her many great ancestors before her, with *gifts* and *talents*. She was what we would call a *full bred,* from a strong uninterrupted bloodline.

It is important to know about Leah's father, though I never actually met him, I knew of him. He was called Dreamer, and was also from a strong bloodline – his father before him, Leah's grandfather, was a *Medicine Man* or if you prefer, a *voodoo priest* from West Africa. He travelled to the USA and met Dreamer's mother, in Salem. She brought her son to England when he was just a boy. Dreamer was extremely *special,* inheriting knowledge and strong *powers* from his African father and unique *gifts* from his mother."

Zoe then paused and took hold of Leah's hand, "Leah, you remind me so much of your beautiful mother, Rose."

Leah's eyes had filled with tears, "Please go on," she said.

Zoe continued, "Shortly, before Rose was murdered by her younger sister, Grace, she asked me to keep you safe, to find you a good family and a new life where you would never discover *who*, or *what* you really are."

Leah stopped her right there, "My aunt murdered my mother? How do you know that for sure?"

Zoe stood silently for a moment, then replied, "Because I was there. So were you, Leah."

Following another pause of shocked silence, Zoe finished her explanation, "Before handing you over to your parents, Pam and William, whom I knew of, through Howard's many, many contacts, I used my gifts of magik one last time. I cast a spell to suppress your *gifts* and to be sure, I cast another one, that you would simply forget anything you might see or do, that could be in any way connected with magik. However, I now see that I have caused you much frustration and suffering."

It was time for Howard to fill in the gaps for their young and frightened *Oracle.*

He began, "Your dreams told us where to find a small golden jewelled box, containing an *eternal flame.* It had been hidden long ago in a field beneath a tree, close to the Temple of Bruer, by an old knight and his son. It is the only fire that can burn and destroy a demon."

Zac's memories of his grandfather, centuries before, taking great care to protect *a flame* circled inside his mind. He also remembered an old monk he had once met and wondered ...

Howard then explained, "Leah, *dear child*, you also warned us at Christmastime that an enemy were preparing to destroy us, here in Lincoln. You described Zachariah and his master to us in your dream."

Leah did not know whether to feel proud, embarrassed or betrayed.

Zoe spoke again, "You are extremely strong and powerful Leah, you can help us if you so choose to? I can reverse my spell, however, the consequences of that might cause you more pain and distress than you could possibly bare right now?"

Everyone remained silent, waiting for Leah's answer.

"I am either some kind of strong and powerful *witch*, or I am too weak to survive another spell, please make up your mind," Leah answered bluntly.

It was Mac who spoke next, "I think I should take Leah to my home," he suggested, "We are going to need every weapon at our disposal and there are many artifacts she might be able to identify for us, just like she did at Christmas."

Zac then interrupted, "I would also be able to help you with that, having been around ... a long time and seen many *instruments of war*. I could also test whether your weapons are *sacred*, or just pretty."

"No way!" Taylor roared, "He's been sent to find out where our weapons are kept!"

Mac argued, "I think he would be useful to us. And there is a way to ensure he cannot betray us, *the chain*?

Stephen added, "Well, we could do with the help, guys, and quickly. We are going to need a hell of a lot of arrows and there are a lot down there, but which ones will work?" he shrugged, dramatically raising his arms up into the air.

Howard had made a decision, "Okay," he began, "Here is what we are going to do. Mac and Taylor, take Leah to the relics at Mac's and take Zac with you – that is if you are willing to be restrained, Zac?"

"Yes, I am," came Zac's instant reply.

"Get as many weapons as you can and bring them back here," Howard continued, "Leah, we are especially seeking *something* that will *sanctify* the ground here; maybe a vessel containing some sort of holy water, or anything like that?"

"Yes, I understand, but is Zoe going to reverse *the spell* first?" Leah asked, "I'm not as confident as you appear to be, that I will be able to do what it is that you want me to."

"No," Howard firmly replied, "Not yet. It is too uncertain how you will deal with the spell reversal. Our priorities must be to get more weapons, especially now we know that practically every demon on Earth is currently heading here, to Lincoln. You were incredible at Christmas, identifying pieces that even Mac and Stephen had never come across before. Although you are wide awake this time, I have faith that you can do this for us again tonight, Leah."

Mac took the golden *mystical chain* from his pocket and walked towards Zac. However, Taylor intercepted him.

"Here," he said, holding out his hand, "Give it to me and I'll restrain our *hero*."

Taylor, looking too smug, wrapped the chain around the top of Zac's chest and arms. Everyone waited in silence.

Zac looked round the circle of expectant faces, "Am I missing something, here?" he asked them, "Aren't I supposed to feel weak, or do a dance, or ... *something?*"

Taylor turned and looked at Mac, "It doesn't work?" stating the obvious.

Howard sighed, "He is not *demonic*, it's clearly useless against him."

"It doesn't matter," said Stephen, "We have weapons that will destroy him if he once steps out of line and he doesn't need to be

141

on *sacred ground* for us to do it, either."

"That's just great!" said Taylor, "We can kill him, but we can't restrain him?"

Now it was Zac who looked back smugly at Taylor.

Zoe stepped forward, "Leah has befriended and trusted Zac, right from the beginning. I also can sense no malice towards us. I think we need to trust him."

A few minutes later, Mac drove his car out of The Forum carpark with Leah beside him in the passenger seat and Taylor and Zac, sitting together in the back.

Mac and Taylor felt good in the knowledge that Howard and Zoe were under the protection of Stephen, Gemma, Jaz, Shania and Sabia, however, Mac still decided to make a quick call to Mahdi and tell him the situation before they left. Mahdi and his warriors would also need to be prepared for the battle ahead.

Leah had expected their journey to take them back into the City, to Mac's *home*. She was surprised when he drove them in a completely different direction. It was dark by now and the bright headlights lit up the ever-winding country roads.

After what had seemed like an extraordinary long time to Leah, Mac began to drive more carefully and slowly along some extremely dark and narrow lanes. It felt like they were travelling through a tunnel, the trees completely closing them in.

Driving down one particular lane, Mac suddenly turned into a gap of high thick hedging. When the car stopped abruptly, a second later, Leah noticed that they had just entered through a large opened wooden gate.

Mac spoke into his handsfree phone, "You can close the gates now. Thank you. I have three occupants with me."

Having driven through yet more winding lanes and crossing a bridge over a small stream, they suddenly pulled up in front of a beautiful country manor house. Lights directed up at the property from around the edges of the wild flowered garden, lit up the most exquisite property of great character. The age of the actual house was certainly much older than the roof and windows. However, unlike Mac's town residence, this was not at all modern inside and its ageless magnetism remained.

An elderly gent, tall and slightly bent over, dressed in a smart expensive suit, white shirt and tie, opened the original wooden front door and greeted them warmly in a deep well-spoken voice, "Come in, my boy! Bring your friends into the warmth. Maria has insisted on staying up and will be excited to see you, she has just put the kettle on!"

Mac stopped inside the hallway, "I am sorry, George, but we do not have the time. I need the keys to the chapel please."

The friendly smile immediately drained from the old man's face and was replaced with a grim and worried expression, "Things must be extremely bad if you turn up at this time of night and need to go down there?"

"It will be alright, George, please don't worry yourself," Mac kindly assured him.

Suddenly, a young attractive woman appeared from one of the many closed doors. She had a voluptuous figure, bright red painted lips, short shiny black hair and she was dressed in a colourful tight-fitting knee-length dress and black patent leather high heeled court shoes.

Thrilled to see Mac, she squealed and then spoke in her strong Italian accent, "Mac, my beautiful boy!"

Maria wrapped her arms around him, and Mac appeared completely comfortable with her closeness and kissed her on her cheek.

"And you have brought some friends to see us?" she exclaimed.

Mac smiled, "Yes. Maria, you know Taylor already, of course and this is Leah and Zac."

Maria beamed at her guests until her eyes fell upon Zac. She suddenly became tense and looked at George for some kind of reassurance.

"It is alright, *my dearest*. Mac is here for the Chapel keys, would you fetch them, please?" George asked her.

Maria turned and disappeared into another room, returning a couple of minutes later clutching an ancient set of iron keys on a large iron ring. She solemnly handed them to Mac, then flung her arms around him once more.

"Please, please be careful my darling boy!" she begged, leaving everyone else present feeling slightly awkward.

"Come now, Maria," said George, "You must allow Mac and his friends to leave, they clearly have an important and difficult night ahead."

Maria took a step back and George opened the door, "Only drive your car as far as the perimeter of the wood, it got terribly drenched last week, and it remains extremely muddy," he warned them.

As everyone headed back towards the car, Leah turned around just in time to see George put a protective arm around Maria and then witnessed Maria take hold of his time-worn wrinkled hand and tenderly kiss it.

Once all were back inside the car, Mac drove around the side of the large property, to the back, where the garden seemed endless and the sounds of large dogs could be heard barking in the distance. A few minutes later, they came to the edge of a woodland.

"Right then," Mac said, "This is where we have to get out and walk I'm afraid."

The temperature had turned freezing and Leah was grateful to have brought her warm gloves and scarf. As they entered the dark wood, stars twinkled above, and gigantic trees swayed in the cold night breeze. On reaching a more tightly packed area of ancient trees and prickly shrubs, walking was becoming more difficult.

Leah suddenly lost her footing and almost fell, Taylor moved swiftly to take her arm but was too late, as Zac arrived first to offer her his support. The two men exchanged childish glares.

Finally, the group reached a clearing, where stood a small brick building with a wooden roof. It resembled an old cattle-shed, with wooden shutters and a sturdy door. Mac used one of the keys from the ring to open it and then, once all were inside, he locked it again.

The tiny chapel was bare but for three rows of old oak benches, a plain unimpressive wooden pulpit stood at the front. The only light inside was that coming from Mac and Taylor's phone-torches.

Leah and Zac watched as Mac and Taylor quietly moved the middle bench to the far right of the small room then using a blunt round-edged blade, lifted a few of the floorboards, revealing a locked trapdoor beneath. Mac used another key to open it, revealing steps leading down, underground.

Mac led the way down the steps, along a narrow tunnel until they arrived at yet another, ancient-looking, locked door. Once again, Mac unlocked it, opening the last barrier to reveal the long cellar, stretching far back into the darkness. He flicked a switch igniting a row of old electric lightbulbs, crudely suspended along the centre of the ceiling and flowing down the entire length of the vast space.

Leah noticed the ancient iron flame-holders hung around the walls. They still contained the long wooden poles topped with rag, probably soaked in a mixture of sulphur and lime, and at one time, would be lit when required by the former *keepers* and *protectors* of this *secret lair*. They had simply remained, having been made redundant once an appropriate electrical generator had been invented during the 1800s.

Leah gazed into the depth of the chamber, filled with heaving shelves, containers and chests filled with treasures: books, ancient scrolls, weapons and jewels. She also observed the different shapes and symbols carved into many of the stones of the walls. She found herself touching, stroking an etching of a pentacle, the five-pointed star, contained within a circle and it made her feel calm and strong. Close by, she found a small marble figure of a female form holding a young child in her arms. She touched the triple moon symbol scratched beneath.

Taylor had noticed her interest, "Ah, The Virgin Mary?" he suggested.

"No, it isn't," she replied, protectively, "It's Mother Earth."

Zac suddenly called from deep within the cellar, "Here! You'll need all of these!"

Leah followed Taylor and Mac to join Zac. They found him with his arms dripping in deep red blood, having sorted weapons that sliced his flesh leaving lacerations that did not miraculously heal. He had been experimenting, cutting himself with the numerous swords, daggers and arrowheads, to have discovered that most of his abrasions would repair themselves. However, he had now assembled a large quantity of *enchanted* weaponry required for the *supernatural battle* ahead.

Leah felt a surge of excitement flow through her body as her elbow touched a small leather pouch, lying on top of a pile of old books.

She immediately picked it up and called to the others, "We will need this, too. Don't ask me why, but we will need it."

Taylor and Mac looked at her questioningly, but Zac recognised it immediately.

"I have seen it before," he revealed, "It's supposed to be given to ... the *Jew, to use, when the time is right*."

Leah removed the unremarkable looking stone from its pouch. Holding it tightly in her hand, she suddenly saw pictures in her mind, of a young man fighting a *demonic* giant of an enemy. She saw him place the stone into a sling, then strike the demon in the centre of his forehead, before cutting off his head with his opponent's own sword.

Leah explained what she could see and *feel* to the others and when she had finished, Mac and Taylor said together, "David and Goliath from The Old Testament!"

Leah then noticed Zac suddenly steady himself.

"Are you okay?" she asked, assisting him to sit upon an old chest close by.

Mac and Taylor turned to discover Leah's concern.

"I feel so weak," he replied, "I hurt all over; I've never experienced this before."

Mac considered the possible causes, then reflected, "This Christian Chapel was built upon *sacred ground*, many, many centuries ago. However, before that, it was a place of Pagan worship, almost since time began. You could not tread upon more *hallowed ground* than here, maybe that is what is *effecting* you somehow, Zac?"

"That's it!" cried Leah, "Now I know how we can make The Forum strong!"

"That is great news, Leah," Taylor said, sounding surprised, then asked simply, "How?"

"Well," she began excitedly, "Howard has tried *blessing* The Forum with priests and religious men and women from all the different practising religions, right?" she questioned them, impatiently pausing for their reply.

"Yes," answered Taylor and Mac together.

"But has it been *blessed* by anyone practising the *oldest religion on Earth*?" Leah asked, becoming more animated by the second.

"No, no, it hasn't," said Mac thoughtfully, "I think I know where you are going with this, Leah. So, who do you think *can bless* the

147

ground of The Forum and protect it against evil, allowing our weapons to destroy the *unearthly souls* of our enemies?"

"Zoe can!" Leah cried, "And ... and ... me, probably, if she can tell me what to do."

"Right then!" Mac began, "Let's each carry some of these weapons back to the car and return to The Forum as quickly as possible. Then I need to contact our Jewish friend, Benjamin, about this *stone.*"

"Let's do it!" said Taylor.

"Here," Zac said, slowly rising to stand whilst showing signs of considerable pain and fatigue, "Take these too."

First he handed Taylor a crumpled-up sheet of red silk, "You could walk through an atomic bomb wrapped in this and not suffer a single burn," he said.

Then he gave him a small tin containing tea leaves, Taylor looked inside the tin and commented, "What do we need this for? I'm not making you a cup of tea when we arrive back at The Forum!"

"It's *Blue Tea,*" Zac replied irritably, "Discovered in the City of Angkor Thom, the Capital of the Khmer Empire during the 1200s, by a Chinese traveller called Chou Ta-Kuan. It makes the drinker invisible for a short time." Taylor looked at Zac apprehensively.

"That's great, thank you," Mac said to him confidently, taking hold of the tin.

Unnoticed by the others, Leah had come across a golden *chalice,* thrown into a box among many others. This one had silently *called* to her. For she was *meant* to own it, she simply *knew* it should belong to *her.* It was luckily small enough to discretely place inside the large pocket of her warm coat.

The following hour was spent taking the supply of weapons up above ground and securing the old chapel again before leaving.

The group, each carrying a part of the precious hoard, made their way back through the shelter of the tall trees and were just a few exhausting paces away from Mac's car, when they were unpleasantly surprised to be met by a nasty and unexpected *welcoming party*.

Infront of Mac's car were parked two impressive motorcycles. Two loathsome looking creatures, dressed in motorbike leathers and boots were stood waiting patiently, ready to greet them.

The short obese one with sores and scabs covering his squashed-up face and round bald head, spoke first, in a German accent, *"Vell, ve vere not expecting to find you here, Zachariah!"*

Next, the other one, who was tall, extremely thin with long greasy hair and extremely small beady eyes added, in the same accent, *"You beat us to zem, did you not, bruzzer?"*

"Well, if it isn't Benny and his adorable side-kick, Miller?" Zac smiled, "Raama is really *scraping the barrel* if he's called you two up!"

Benny was clearly dubious and suspicious of the situation, but Miller laughed at what he naively believed was a joke.

Leah, Taylor and Mac were feeling extremely nervous; they were completely exposed, carrying the *precious weapons* and their only means of protecting the future of The Forum. Had they all been deceived by Zac? Maybe his clever *act* had successfully manipulated Leah into giving him access to *them* and their *secrets*, just as he and Raama had planned in the beginning?

The following few minutes would reveal, who exactly, were to be the *betrayed*.

TRAITORS

The stand-off, just a few feet away from Taylor's car, was becoming more tense as Benny and Miller glared back at Mac, Taylor, Leah and Zac, all heavily laden with weaponry.

"*So, vot is it zat you are actually doing here, Zachariah?*" Benny questioned suspiciously.

"Waiting for you to finally turn up," Zac answered, sarcastically, "It has taken you long enough!"

Taylor exchanged angry glances with Mac, however Mac then gave Taylor a *knowing nod*, as if to reassure him that events might not be as bad as they presently seemed.

Zac spoke again, this time to Mac and Taylor, "Put the weapons into the car and take these from me!"

He handed over his armful of weaponry to Taylor, who had been first to place his own into the car's boot. Zac had with-held a small jewel-handled knife.

"Be ready," he whispered to Taylor.

"*Shall ve kill zem now?*" Miller asked hopefully.

"In a minute," Zac replied, "We will take the girl to Raama, she is a powerful witch, she'll be easily *turned* and of good use to him."

Directing his eyes to Leah, he ordered, "Get into the back seat, now!" Leah obediently did as she was instructed, completely trusting Zac's motives.

Once Leah was safe inside the car, along with their mystical load, Benny and Miller watched, intrigued, as Zac then walked towards them. In a blink of an eye, he had grabbed them both by their throats, one in each powerful hand and had them swinging off the ground. He bashed them together like a huge pair of brass band symbols, the impact being so forceful, they were immediately flung to the ground in a daze.

"Go!" Zac yelled to the others.

Mac ran and jumped into the driver's seat.

Taylor hesitated a second, "I'll stay and help you, Zac!"

"Are you worried about me, Taylor?" Zac smirked, "That's really *touching*!" Then he continued, more genuinely, this time, "These are *second rate*, I will be fine. I'll meet you back at The Forum soon."

"Okay," responded Taylor, "If you are sure." Then he jumped into the passenger seat as Mac reversed and then drove away hastily.

Leaving the dramatic scene, Leah was surprised at Mac's conversation as he immediately made a call, whilst driving expertly back towards the Manor House.

"Hi George! We had unexpected visitors. Zac is still at the boundary and might need Maria's assistance," he said.

George's voice was then heard, loud and clear to all inside the car.

"Alright, Mac. Maria is here with me now. I have opened the Main Gate for you. Be careful, *my boy*."

Next, Maria's strong Italian voice spoke, "I will go there with *the puppies* immediately Mac. Don't worry, I will call *a friend* to secure the breach of the property's boundary." Then she asked him, "How many are there?"

"Thank you, there are two, that I know of," replied Mac.

Maria spoke again, as Mac's car raced through the opened Main Gate and headed back towards Lincoln, "Please, please be careful, Mac. We love you so, so very much!"

Mac answered, "I will Mum. You take care too. And ... I love you very much as well. Please don't worry."

Taylor could see the puzzled expression across Leah's face from his front seat mirror, "You might need to explain your *unique* and *happy little family* to Leah, Mac," he said.

Mac smiled at her through his own mirror, "Okay, where should I begin? Well, I was sent away to a boarding school at the age of five until I was a teenager, and spent all of the holidays with George and Maria in different locations each year. I believed they were my real parents, that George had been a butler for Lord and Lady Kingstone. When they were all younger, before I was born, they had travelled across the world, experiencing dangerous and exciting adventures together. Shortly after I was born, Lord and Lady Kingstone were killed, in an accident. I discovered when I was sixteen that they were my *real* parents and that they had actually been murdered. I would have died along with them if George and Maria had not decided to take me out for a walk in my pram, just moments earlier. The papers announced that Lord and Lady Kingstone, along with their baby son, had *all* died in the explosion."

"Wow!" Leah muttered.

Mac continued with his story, "When the will was read, everything had been left to George and he and Maria brought me up as their own son. I took his surname of 'Mckenna'. George legally signed everything back over to me when I was eighteen, he also had a lot of other *secrets* to divulge to me."

"I can imagine!" Leah replied, completely amazed and intrigued. "So," she began, "You are actually the *real* heir?"

"Yes!" It was Taylor who had replied, as they turned onto the brighter lit road, leading them back towards The Forum, "Leah," he continued proudly, "You are privileged to be in the company of Lord Jasper Kingstone, himself!"

Mac then added hastily, "However, the fewer people that know this story, the better."

"Of course." Leah replied thoughtfully, then enquired, "Mac, Maria looks so much younger than George, how can that be?"

"Oh yes," Mac laughed, "Sorry, I missed the best bit out! Maria is like your friend, Zachariah; she was *turned* into an *immortal* at the age of twenty, around the time George was actually born. They met on one of George and my parents' adventures in Italy. Their story would be a fictional-romance novelist's dream! They have also been wonderful parents to me."

"Does Shania know?" Leah asked.

"Yes," came Mac's immediate reply.

Meanwhile, back at The Forum, Howard, Zoe, Stephen, Gemma, Shania, Jaz and Sabia were awaiting any news from the others. They were instantly relieved when they watched Mac's car drive into the carpark and pull up outside. Once the *Facial Recognition Monitor* confirmed all was well, they rushed to greet them, then assisted to bring the treasures inside.

"What has happened to Zac?" asked Howard.

"A couple of his *old chums* turned up uninvited," Taylor answered.

"He helped us to find the *sanctified weapons* and to escape," Mac added, "Hopefully, he will be joining us shortly."

Back in the woods of the Kingstone Estate, Zac had faced his former *associates,* now fully recovered from the unexpected act of aggression from their *comrade.* The enraged couple were now preparing to take their revenge.

A fight commenced. Benny and Miller were strong and powerful, though clumsy and they proved inept in the contest against Zachariah. Miller was first to be destroyed at the hands of Zac, by the mystical knife he had kept for himself from the chapel. Benny, heavier and more experienced in combat, had taken a little longer to defeat and had drained more of Zachariah's energy, already sapped by the powers and forces he had felt within the ancient sanctuary.

Benny's wicked soul had finally been successfully extinguished upon the hallowed ground of The Kingstone Estate, and the knife remained lying in the middle of the pile of black ashes, once his body.

Zac wearily stood and then rested his aching body against the trunk of an ancient oak tree. Foolishly, he closed his tired eyes for just a second.

A sudden and unbearable pain shot through his shoulder and Zac realised he had been pinned to the tree by the same *enchanted knife* he had used on Miller and Benny. He looked up to see a beautiful but deadly female face that he immediately recognised.

The stunningly desirable and seductive daughter of Evil stood directly before him. She stood close enough to touch Zac, but far away enough to step back, should she need to.

"Well, aren't you a naughty boy?" she purred, watching the blood flow from her captive's shoulder. She touched his full lips with her middle finger, then put it gently into his mouth. She stroked the tip of his dry tongue, then put her finger into her own mouth, erotically savouring his taste.

Zac fought the urge to resist, instead choosing to avoid the loss of more blood or energy.

"Sibyl," he uttered finally, "It has been a long time since we last met."

Sybil laughed, "Yes, it has been a couple of centuries and clearly, a lot has happened to you since then. I just watched you destroy Miller and Benny. I suppose I should have stepped in to help them really, but it was too much fun watching those fools perish at your gorgeous hands!"

Noticing his failing strength and the effects of the knife, Sibyl stepped forward and kissed him hard, before savagely biting his lip. His supernatural body attempted to heal the wound and slowly began to mend itself. Again, Sybil smiled before suddenly pulling the knife out of Zac's shoulder, releasing him and allowing his body to slump wearily to the ground. She bent down beside him then cut his bottom lip with the knife, blood trickled down his strong masculine chin. She was fascinated by the knife's ability to harm the *unharmable.*

Without warning, Zac suddenly grabbed hold of her wrist, wrestled the knife out of her hand and threw it into the trees. He was still incredibly weak and let out a moan of excruciating pain when Sybil managed to powerfully kick his wounded shoulder hard against the trunk of the tree.

The following second, the unexpected loud and shocking sound of excitable vicious hounds could be heard coming closer. Their terrifying howls were not of this world and the earth-shaking vibrations of their heavy paws landing upon the woodland were becoming greater.

Sybil jumped to her feet and stood still, listening for a few seconds before running back into the dense woodland, in the opposite direction of the approaching petrifying sound.

Zac was slowly losing consciousness, but recognised Maria as she emerged from behind some trees, holding his knife and surrounded by a pack of at least twenty incredibly large cross-bred dogs. However, these creatures were no-longer mortal canine pets but *unearthly beasts* of powerful supernatural muscle, teeth and claws.

On Maria's command, her *puppies* fell silent and formed a ring of awesome protection around her and Zac. She knelt beside him and took out a bottle of water and a small tin containing an oil, from a bag hung around her shoulder. Zac gratefully sipped the water she gave him while Maria gently soothed the oil around his wounds.

Zac watched her, then spoke softly, "They have weapons to destroy us and they also have oils to heal us?"

Maria smiled as she gently stroked his torn lip with the soothing oil, "You are not the first demon to switch sides and hopefully, you won't be the last either."

A few minutes later, Zac had regained some of his strength and his wounds were slowly but surely healing.

"Thank you," he said, taking a few last sips of the cool water, "When did you ... *switch sides?*" he asked her.

Maria helped Zac to his feet, "I was a young waitress in my father's café, when I met *him, Actaeon.* I was a vain foolish girl and he first became my lover, then when he *turned* me and gave me immortality, he became my cruel master, who treated me as badly as he did these beautiful creatures."

Maria looked around at the pack, then continued, "When I met George, along with the Kingstones, I knew I had to help them in their quest for good. Instead of obeying my master, Actaeon and killing *them,* I destroyed *him* instead. I instantly fell in love with George the moment I set eyes upon him. I now cherish my family. George and Mac have given me more happiness than I deserve. I have tried to make amends for all the bad things I once did, and I believe I have been a good wife and mother. These beautiful *puppies* have a kind mistress to love them now, for always, just as all puppies deserve."

As if her hounds had understood her words, they turned their heads and looked at her for a brief second, before returning to their guarding duties. Two, came to sit by her side, allowing her to pet them.

"What will you do when George dies?" Zac asked of her.

Maria's eyes glazed and became watery as she replied, "I will continue to assist the Kingstones and their descendants. I will help them to protect their chapel and the many secrets of their ancestors, the Knights of Temple Bruer."

"But the Kingstone bloodline was destroyed over twenty years ago?" Zac questioned, "My master, Raama, was responsible."

Maria laughed indignantly, "Your master is not as clever, or as important, as he thinks he is!" And with this, she accompanied Zac to where the two motorcycles stood waiting. "Now go and help *my precious boy* and his friends," she instructed, "Do what is right, Zachariah. You also deserve to find some peace and happiness."

Maria's words were now etched into Zac's mind as he rode back towards Lincoln.

Do what is right ... You also deserve peace and happiness.

Back at The Forum, Mac and Taylor left Leah to explain the various *weapons* and *mystical pieces* to the others, while they headed directly for the IT Suite upstairs. Once secured inside the classroom, the large interactive whiteboard at the front, became a screen. Taylor sat at a table at the back of the room and opened a secret compartment containing a sophisticated tablet.

Having input some information, the face of a young man, around the age of seventeen, with smart short black hair and wearing large framed glasses, appeared on the whiteboard.

"Hi Taylor! Oh, is that Mac I can see there with you?" the boy, gifted with autism and extreme intelligence, was delighted to see his friends.

Taylor and Mac waved, "Hi Benjamin," then Taylor explained, "We need your help again, *Buddy*."

Benjamin rubbed his hands together, "Super!" he exclaimed, "Fire away!"

Just then, Benjamin's mother called up the stairs to him, in his bedroom, "Benji! You haven't told me what you wanted for your supper yet? I'm not a mind reader! It's no good telling me you're hungry then not eating what I make for you, just like you did again last night! *I have things I need ta do too, you know!"*

"I'm busy right now, Mum!" he yelled back, irritably, then returned his attention to his friends. "What do you need from me, today guys?"

Benjamin's mother called out again, "Benji! Benji! Did you want the left-over turkey from dinner? Anyway, do you know how late it is? You should be going to bed not eating at this time of night!"

Benjamin lost his temper, "Mum! Be quiet!"

"Don't you talk to ya mother in that tone of voice!"

"I'm helping Taylor and Mac! We have to save the world, Mum!" Benjamin shouted.

A short silence followed, then her voice, much sweeter now, called back, "Why didn't you just say so? Give them my love!"

Benjamin regained his calmer self, "Okay Mum!"

"Good boy!"

"Mum!"

"Yes Benji?"

"Could I please have the turkey in a white toastie with pickle?" he asked thoughtfully.

"I'll go and make it for you now, Benji!" his mother responded happily.

"So, let's get down to business, guys!" Benjamin said enthusiastically.

Mac, who had been waiting patiently, could now speak, "We have in our possession a stone. We have been told today that it is ... *for the Jew to use when the time is right.* Does that mean anything to you?

"I'm Jewish!" said Benjamin, proudly, "So are my Mum and Dad!"

"Yes, we know you are, Benjamin," Mac replied, "Could you do a little research for us please? Now?"

"Sure!" Benjamin nodded, sliding his chair away from the screen, allowing Mac and Taylor to once again, appreciate just how many computers and other ingenious pieces of technology can be squeezed into the space of a teenage boys' bedroom.

A few minutes later, Benjamin's face returned onto the large screen, "The stone belonged to David, from The Old Testament, who placed the stone through a sacred flame, before using it to defeat a demon called Goliath."

"The *flame*?" questioned Mac.

"Yeah," Benjamin answered, sounding a little bored, "You've already got that haven't you? You should try putting your small arrowheads and bullets through it. It's a form of *spiritual baptism* for blades, objects and ... *stuff.*"

"Wow!" Taylor continued, "But are we supposed to give the stone to somebody Jewish to use? What does **when the time is right** mean?"

Benjamin laughed, "You crazy guys! That's easy! The **time** is now because you just found it! And you must already know who the **Jew** is, probably from the bloodline of David. **They** must use it to destroy your strongest opposition. If you didn't have the *Jew,* you wouldn't have found *David's Stone* yet, would you? These things don't just happen without a reason, you know!"

Mac and Taylor looked at one another in shock, Taylor spoke first, "It's Zachariah! It has to be! It must be *him* who uses *David's Stone* to destroy Raama! But where is he and do you think he will do it when the time comes?"

Benjamin's voice interrupted them, "I'm going to go now, I want my supper! Bye guys! Don't get killed!"

Mac and Taylor smiled, "Bye Benjamin!"

"And thank you, once again!" Mac called, as Benjamin's smiling mother could now be seen on the screen. She was entering her son's bedroom holding a toasted sandwich on a plate in one hand, while frantically waving back at them, with the other.

Benjamin's face suddenly disappeared, and the screen went black.

Shortly after, Mac and Taylor headed back downstairs to the others, where a conversation had begun.

Zoe was speaking, "It makes sense, Howard. Don't you see? Leah is right! We need to *bless* The Forum now, so it is upon *hallowed ground.* Then the *weapons* can do their job and destroy the *unearthly souls.* But the *blessing* will need to be powerful and strong, I will need Leah's help."

"Of course," Leah replied, "But first, please, please release your spell that you put on me as an infant."

Choosing not to answer Leah just at that moment, Zoe turned to look at one of the knights, "And, we could do with your help too, Gemma," she said.

Everyone turned, looking bewildered at Gemma. Stephen was particularly alarmed.

Gemma was devastated and begged, "No! Zoe, please don't!"

Stephen walked over to his wife's side, "What is going on, here?" he asked warily, looking from Zoe, then back to Gemma.

Gemma closed her eyes, then took a deep breath. After a moment of silent thought, she looked up again at Zoe, "How long have you known?" she asked her coldly.

Zoe replied, "Since the first time Stephen brought you to meet us. I felt it instantly, so I did a little research. You come from a bloodline of *witches,* but many of your ancestors have chosen to follow their heart and bred with *ordinary folk.* Your mother, and her mother, chose *love* over the *bloodline.* I believed that I should give you a chance before I let your secret out."

Gemma was distraught, "I only found out a few years ago. I was a child prodigy, able to learn a new language fluently within a couple of weeks, so I always knew I was *special*. Growing up in foster care wasn't the best start in life for a kid, but as I grew up and my skills were recognised, I was placed into the care of a Professor at the university and my career began there, at an extremely young age. I was contacted by someone here in the UK a couple of years ago. This woman told me that my foremothers were all *dark witches* and that she could help me discover my other true *gifts*. She said that she needed my help to bring down a group of people who were becoming a problem among her community – my *own people*, where she said I *belonged*."

Zoe interrupted, "Was this woman's name, Grace, by any chance?"

"Yes, it was," Gemma replied.

Stephen began to shake his head, "You'd had it all planned, that day we met, hadn't you?" Becoming angrier, he continued, "You staged the whole thing! Everyone was so shocked and thrilled to be having this world famous young American Language Professor, travel across the ocean to lecture at our *humble little university*. And that day, in the canteen, you *played* me, didn't you? And I fell for it!"

Stephen was visibly heartbroken.

Gemma became hysterical, "Please, please Stephen, just listen to me! I did come to England intending to find a way into the inner circle of The Forum. I admit that! And, yes, I did plan to use you as a way in! But Stephen, then I fell deeply in love with you! You are my world now, my reason to wake up every morning and to breathe. You're my husband and I want us to have children and a future together! I swear, I have deliberately avoided any recent contact with Grace and have not given her any further information or secrets about us, or about Howard and The Forum."

Jaz suddenly joined the heated discussion, "That night, in the carpark, when Howard and Zoe were attacked by a demon, you *deliberately* dropped the chain that might have freed him, didn't you?"

Zoe spoke softly, "None of you were meant to make it out into the carpark in time to save us, were you, Gemma? You were *struggling* with a particular manoeuvre that Jaz was teaching you all on that night, as I recall."

"I'm so sorry," Gemma cried, "I am different now! I love what The Forum stands for, what it does! And I love all of you! I will spend the rest of my life proving it and protecting you, I swear!"

Taylor explained, solemnly, "Gemma, if any one of us doesn't respond to a *distress signal* either on our phone or watch, set off by a security device from any of our protected locations, I get a warning, just below my ear." He stroked a small unnoticeable scar in the area of his neck and ear, "That's how I knew something was wrong and we reached Howard and Zoe just in time, even though we weren't wearing any of our devices during that particular training session."

"Can you ever forgive me, any of you?" Gemma pleaded with them all, "Stephen, if you are willing to give me a chance, I will prove my loyalty to you and to everyone else at The Forum."

Zoe turned to Stephen, who was angry and hurt, to explain, "Stephen, Gemma is not lying, she loves you with all of her heart. When a *witch* truly falls in love, she loves with all of her soul, for the rest of her life and she can prove her loyalty now, to all of us. She can help Leah and I to *purify* this place?"

Suddenly, every warning sound in the building erupted. Shania ran to the windows and peered outside, while the others prepared themselves. The sun was rising, and the carpark was filling with vehicles loaded with the enemy.

It then came appallingly apparent that the first line of *dispensable soldiers*, jealous and hateful mortals, armed with bats, knives and other nasty crude weapons, were already inside the building! The battle had begun!

ENEMIES

Taylor checked his monitor to see the mortal army advance through the shattered doors of the entrance to The Forum. At least fifty armed thugs, male and female, rioted angrily through, into the dining area.

The angry mob stampeded towards the knights and a nasty and difficult fight erupted. The knights did not want to kill *this* enemy, of foolish flesh and blood. Yet the easily manipulated horde, were intent on butchering *them* with their amateurish yet sharp and deadly weapons.

Sabia, Amir and the knights, formed a protective circle around Howard, Zoe and Leah, constantly shielding them from the endless deadly strikes. The *sacred armour* was deflecting the relentless stabs and the sheer skill and ability of each knight was a magnificent sight to behold.

As the numbers of the pathetic mob decreased, either having been adeptly stricken unconscious or from falling to the ground from sheer exhaustion, the knights were able to successfully restrain each and every one. Now, each secured by a thin resilient cord and confined to the dining area, they were suddenly in the midst of a bombardment of flamed fuelled arrows, breaking the glass and shooting through the windows.

"Quick! Get them over to the sides! They'll be burned alive!" Howard commanded.

Amir proved himself a great addition to *the team*, using his size, strength and intelligence to assist in the dragging of every unconscious prisoner out of harm's way.

The Forum was now experiencing the *second wave* of Raama's attack.

A few hundred demons had surrounded the entire building. Some were hideous looking while others were visually beautiful. Deadly arrows and silent bullets were pouring in through the windows. Stephen tried shooting back at a few of the closest enemy, but they instantly recovered, as had been predicted.

"Get this place *blessed*, Howard, or we're all going to die!" Stephen called.

Gemma and Sabia, now with Amir at her side, ushered Howard, Zoe and Leah back down towards The Main Hall, "We must get the ground *hallowed*, so our *weapons* are effective and ready for the second attack!" Gemma said. Once inside the Main Hall she locked the doors, "What do we do, Zoe?"

Zoe looked troubled, "We need to be outside, actually treading on the soil," she answered, "I don't know how we are going to do it."

"I am not allowing you to go outside!" Howard stated firmly. "We are surrounded, you wouldn't live long enough to complete the *blessing*."

Leah spoke now, "Make me strong, Zoe," she said, "Release my powers, please?"

Zoe looked to Howard for his approval, "Do it!" he instructed.

Under the watchful eyes of Howard, Sabia and Gemma, Leah knelt before Zoe. Zoe began by asking the *Spirits and Powers of the Universe* to hear her request. Then she began speaking in an *unearthly* language only Gemma could vaguely understand.

The air surrounding them became cold, then hot. Howard, Gemma, Sabia and Amir were suddenly overcome with unbearable pain as a loud whistle shot through their eardrums. Amir curled up into a big ball of fluff, whimpering, while everyone else placed their hands over their ears and closed their eyes throughout their moment long agony. They opened them again to discover Leah laying on the floor.

Leah appeared to have a fever and was experiencing terrifying hallucinations. Her cries of grief, sadness and terror were evidence of the countless repressed and rebellious powers, memories, knowledge and *gifts,* now finally released and abruptly exposed to her.

Outside of The Forum, Mahdi, Rafi and Eshan had arrived with other Warriors. They had joined forces with the knights, attacking from behind their enemy, along the far perimeter of the battleground. They used agile and sophisticated bows, with *ancient mystical* arrowheads and were protected by wearing the same *miraculous black cloth* as the knights. The style of their uniforms differed by the longer flared military coats, baggy Harem pants tight at the ankles and turbans, protecting their heads. Each warrior also had a scimitar strapped to their waist.

Eshan and Rafi had attempted to get closer to the building, to protect it from the front, but had suddenly found themselves circled by a group of six vicious demons. These two brave young men each placed their bows around an arm and shoulder, then grabbed his scimitar. Fearlessly, they fought their aggressors, but their weapons could only wound and delay the fiends momentarily. They were deeply surprised and relieved when Zachariah suddenly appeared and joined their incessant fight.

Meanwhile, back inside the Main Hall, Leah was now fully conscious and *forever changed.* She knew what she must do.

The others followed her out into the dining area. Shania and Mac were attempting to put out small fires scattered all over the place, while Stephen, Jaz and Taylor were firing futile bullets from the windows.

"I need the *Blue Tea of Invisibility,*" Leah announced, "We three must reach the trees and grassland behind the building un-detected before we will be able to start the spell which will *sanctify* the grounds."

Gemma and Zoe looked nervously at one another as Leah con-tinued, "I suggest that Howard, you begin cleansing as much *or-dinary* ammunition as you have by passing it through the *flame*. There are more demons on their way. Many, many, more," she warned, "You'll need everything you've got, to fire at this *scum*."

A couple of minutes later, Shania had prepared the *Blue Tea* and having drank a few drops each, Leah, Zoe and Gemma were in-deed completely invisible.

To their advantage, Zachariah, Rafi and Eshan were running up the steps as the *three witches* were coming down, so the move-ment and sounds of broken glass beneath their feet were well masked.

As Leah passed Zachariah, a jolt of energy passed between them and he knew she was there, then she was gone.

Zachariah, Rafi and Eshan were welcomed into The Forum. Rafi and Eshan stood absolutely still in shock, on seeing Sabia inside, dressed as a knight. She was defending herself against a large male demon who had grabbed her through a broken window and would easily have killed her with his knife, if she had not been so incredibly swift, agile and skilled.

She turned, saw them and waved. Then, "Move!" she suddenly yelled. They did, immediately, thus avoiding a petrol bomb thrown in through a nearby window.

Zac found Howard in the kitchen with a table full of bullets and arrowheads that he was placing through the changing coloured *flame* of red, gold and white, burning within a small golden jew-elled box.

He watched silently a moment before confronting him, "What do you want me to do, Howard?" he asked.

"There is nothing any one of us can do but try to stay alive,"

Howard replied grimly, "Until the ground beneath and around The Forum is *sanctified* and our weapons become operational, we are useless against them."

Howard was frightened as he had never been before. Since meeting Zoe, the love of his life, he had wanted to protect her, to make her happy; she was the most important person in his life, and he knew he could never adore another. Now, he feared he risked losing her.

It had just occurred to Howard that Zoe had given up her family, her friends and her *gifts* for him; he had never once questioned himself whether he had the right to ask her to leave her own *religion and lifestyle,* in favour of his. Life, experience, bloodline and secret recently discovered scrolls, had all taught him that

Religion was not the reason behind war and destruction, people were!

Howard had discovered that we were all born to be different and that was exactly how it was meant to be. He came to understand, that all religions teach of love, charity and peace, but all religions also breed those individuals who desire the opposite. How angry it made him feel, that *those people* used their religion and God, as an excuse for their own greed, jealousy, weaknesses and failings. His beautiful, kind and loving wife would once have probably been another victim of those weak and pathetic men born throughout history, who were intimidated and jealous of intelligent and gifted women.

Only God knows how many medical and scientific discoveries have been lost or delayed, due to the persecution and suppression of the female sex or anyone different from the others, he had so often thought to himself.

At that moment, Taylor left his position to go and speak to Howard. He acknowledged Zac, then assured his worried uncle, "Zoe, Gemma and Leah, will do it, Howard. I know they will."

Having carefully manipulated their way around the ever-growing number of demons, to get to the area of trees and green grass, Zoe, Gemma and Leah took off their footwear and joined their hands together, forming a small circle. They *chanted* for a few seconds, independently, before Leah suddenly without warning, broke their chain. She took out the small *chalice* she had taken from the chapel and had kept concealed in her coat pocket.

"Could I borrow a blade, please?" she asked Gemma, who complied and took a small knife from within a fold of her sleeve and then placed it gently into Leah's waiting right hand. Leah then proceeded to cut her left hand, allowing her deep red blood to drip into the mouth of the chalice.

As if this whole scenario had been planned and rehearsed many times before, Zoe, Gemma and Leah began *chanting* in the *unearthly supernatural language* of their *craft*.

Massive raging storm clouds appeared in the skies above. Then, as Leah poured her blood from the *chalice* onto the natural earth, the ground beneath their feet turned red.

Powerful bolts of lightning-strikes could be seen shooting across the carpark and upon the roof of The Forum. The clouds above began to release drops of red rain. One last mighty lightening-strike ended in silence.

The sky cleared, the grass beneath their feet returned to the colour of green and The Forum appeared bright and lit up, in the morning sunshine.

Raama and his army had not witnessed anything like this in centuries. All had stood perfectly still, watching the changing skies and wondering who was responsible for this *ancient magik*.

Suddenly ...

"They've done it! My bullet just destroyed one of them!" Shania yelled.

Following this fantastic announcement, demons were falling and becoming heaps of dust as the *mystical* bullets and arrowheads impaled their victims.

Mac yelled to Howard, "Give the extra arrowheads and blades to Sabia, Eshan and Rafi, we are going outside!"

"I am coming with you!" Sabia roared, then commanded Amir to "Stay!" Placing her bow down beside Eshan and withdrawing her sword.

Eshan could not believe his eyes, as he watched Sabia run after Mac, Shania, Taylor, Stephen and Jaz, with a sword in one hand and a dagger in the other, outside into an almighty raging battle.

Now, finally, the knights could use their *sacred* weapons to destroy their *unearthly* opponents and the secret unique training, plus their incredible skills, could be expended.

Rafi and Eshan, relentlessly firing the miraculous arrows, were amazed watching Sabia fight fearlessly and expertly, along-side the knights.

Mahdi, fighting outside, had known about Sabia's private combat training since Jaz had contacted him, asking for his agreement to teach Sabia the *secret techniques* from the Templar Knights' *ancient scrolls*. He had voiced his opinion that having known Sabia since childhood, he did not consider her an *appropriate candidate* for *this* training. However, he had later reluctantly given Jaz his consent, following Musad's almost fatal attack upon her. He was now impressed, yet slightly concerned, to see Sabia's remarkable combat skills out on the battlefield.

Mahdi, alongside his own warriors, fought together with the knights, in the quest to successfully eliminate a seamlessly, never ending army of demons.

Howard had handed the small leather pouch to Zac, "Here," he said, "Take *David's Stone*. We believe it is meant for *you* to use."

Zac took it and headed outside, wielding the same knife that had caused him so much agony on the *sacred* Kingstone Estate earlier. He was careful to avoid the flying arrows, expertly shot from Mahdi and his warriors from the far end of the carpark. Thankfully, they were quick to acknowledge him fighting on their own side, as he powerfully destroyed one loathsome demon after another.

Howard was now expertly firing his gun from a window. Once all the arrowheads had been depleted, Rafi and Eshan ran outside to continue their fight using their scimitars. The skills and extraordinary abilities of the knights and of the warriors, were magnificent.

One by one, each *evil soul* was extinguished, however, the numbers were constantly renewed as reinforcements continued to arrive.

Eventually, the sheer number of demons were noticeably beginning to dwindle. Gemma used her invisibility to her advantage and was able to wipe out many of the enemy unnoticed. She had chosen to fight alongside Stephen and together they were a formidable team.

She had felt great joy when he had called to her, "That's my girl!" and "You are awesome, *my love!*"

The *Fiendish Army* were clearly losing, and their numbers were few, so Gemma decided to now return to Zoe and Leah and lead them back to the safety of The Forum. Unfortunately, as they approached the steps, the *invisibility charm* began to weaken.

Gemma was suddenly grabbed from behind; the collar of her protective coat was viciously ripped open before she was stabbed. She collapsed to the floor as Zoe and Leah were each grabbed by a strong assailant and dragged to stand directly in front of The Forum.

Howard had witnessed it all from the window and watched in horror, as his beloved Zoe, was restrained by the *Daughter of Evil*, Sibyl. Raama could clearly be seen holding Leah tightly and painfully, by the back of her neck.

Suddenly, all combat ceased.

"Tell them to lay down their weapons, Preacher!" Raama

yelled, "And come outside!"

"Don't do it, Howard!" Jaz called out, "We have things under control!"

Stephen, on noticing his wife, lying bleeding at the foot of the steps, immediately ran to her side.

Raama laughed and then held Leah agonisingly off of the ground, "**Tell them to lay down their weapons and come outside, Preacher!**" he roared once more.

Suddenly, to Raama's surprise, Zac appeared and was walking towards him.

"Stop right there!" Raama commanded him. Zac stood still, his eyes meeting with Leah's. He could see the pain and fear in them and desperately wanted to end her suffering.

"You disappoint me, Zachariah," Raama said bitterly. "You have betrayed me, your master, for what? For *this*?" He flung Leah roughly to the ground.

Sybil was smiling as she smugly held Zoe's arms behind her back. Looking upon Leah, lying face down on the ground, she scorned, "Oh Zachariah, really? This *piece of pathetic human flesh* was enough to *turn you*?"

Raama spoke again, "Tell your new friends to put down their weapons, Zachariah! They may well be able to destroy the remainder of our army, but they cannot destroy *me*, I am a *legitimate Son of Evil*, not a mere demon. They cannot win, surely you know that much? I gave you the *gift of eternal life*, Zachariah, and I can just as easily take it back!"

Zac stared at Raama defiantly, "I have walked this earth for far too long, obeying you, my master. I am well prepared to end my pitiful existence here today and place my soul into the hands of the God my parents once prayed to."

Raama laughed out loud, "Yes! And remember what good that did for them both?" he roared, "Your God will throw you to the depths of Hades!"

Zac replied calmly, "I am already there and have been, since the day I first saw you."

Raama's expression turned to fury. The next moment he began speaking in a loud *supernatural language*, chanting and pointing at Zac.

Zac fell to his knees in excruciating agony, as his whole body began to burn up. When flames appeared to dance around his torso, Leah started *chanting* and begging the *Spirits of the Earth* to help him. Suddenly, she felt a powerful energy inside of her soul and was *spiritually guided* to fire her own anger, power and magik, directly towards Raama.

Staring up at Rama, Leah screamed in a language she had never before known or heard spoken. Raama appeared to weaken. Zoe was then able to break free from Sybil, as the powerful *spell* was affecting her strength also.

As the flames burned stronger, using all of his strength and will, Zac took the small leather pouch from his pocket and took hold of *the stone*. Using the small pouch and its leather tie, as a sling, he aimed and fired *David's Stone* at Raama's head, shooting him between the eyes.

Raama looked shocked and mortified, feeling its impact and catastrophic effect.

As Raama fell to his knees, Mac suddenly appeared from out of nowhere and cut off his head with his sword. Raama, *a son of Evil*, instantly became a pile of dust and was no more.

Running out from The Forum, Howard immediately headed to Zac's side, holding the mystical red silk sheet. Throwing it over Zac's scorching body, he, Mahdi and Taylor began patting out the raging flames.

Once again, the battle resumed. In the euphoric chaos of the final triumphant few moments, Sybil was able to escape unnoticed.

With a multitude of dust-piles, now propelling around in the breeze, turning the air brown, Leah ran to where Zac was lying, surrounded by Howard, Mahdi and Taylor. As she knelt down, Taylor gently lifted the red silk off of Zac's concealed body and peeked beneath, he looked up and smiled at her.

Zac began peeling the silk off himself and sat up. Within seconds, he felt fit, strong and renewed. He smiled back at the four relieved faces and felt reassured by the calm silence surrounding him. They all stood up and walked over to where the knights had surrounded Gemma.

"How is she?" Howard asked Shania, who looked deeply concerned.

"Doc is trying to stop the blood flow until an ambulance arrives. He will go with her to the hospital, with Stephen, who is presently inside getting changed," she replied.

Howard could now see Gemma, lying in Zoe's arms while Eshan, known as *Doc* to the knights, was busy attending her wound.

Within minutes, an ambulance arrived, shortly followed by an unmarked police car. Robyn stepped out from her vehicle and had a few brief words with Howard before walking over to Jaz.

"Are you okay?" she asked her.

"Yes, I am," Jaz reassured her, "It was pretty *intense* here for a while though."

Moments later, both women suddenly noticed the line of unsavoury looking characters, filing out of the building, escorted by the knights and warriors. They looked dazed and confused as they headed for their vehicles, scattered around the carpark. None of them could remember *why* they had come, or for *what* purpose. They just remembered having had a nice cup of tea with chocolate biscuits, that the *kind and beautiful lady called Zoe*, had given them and that now, *they desperately wanted to get back to their homes and sleep off their almighty headaches?*

"I am not even going to ask!" Robyn said to Jaz, shaking her head.

"Best you don't," Jaz smiled.

Sabia, unseen by Robyn, was with Eshan behind the ambulance. Gemma had been connected to a plastic tube and carefully carried on a stretcher inside the vehicle. Stephen was holding her limp hand.

"Will she be okay?" Sabia asked him.

"I hope so," Eshan replied, then added, "I would never have guessed that you ..."

Sabia interrupted him, "I never knew about you and Rafi either; I suppose we both have a lot to learn about one another, don't we?"

"Would you allow me to come and see you at your home one day soon?" Eshan asked hopefully, climbing into the back of the ambulance.

"Yes, I would like that, very much," Sabia replied, with a smile. Then with Amir at her side, she watched the ambulance, followed by Robyn's car, drive away. Afterwards, she found her brother, Rafi and gave him a hug. Mahdi saw them together and all returned smiles and a respectful acknowledgement of a job, well done.

CHAMPIONS

It had been a strange afternoon, as various workers came and went, carrying out the necessary work on the damaged areas of The Forum.

Most of the scheduled classes and meetings were still being held; going ahead as usual, as if nothing extraordinary had ever happened there, just a few hours previously.

Howard and Zoe were sat together with the knights, in their training studio. However, no training sessions were taking place now and they were enjoying their mugs of tea, coffee and hot chocolate whilst helping themselves to the large plate of chocolate biscuits.

All turned as Stephen entered, "How is Gemma doing?" Mac asked immediately.

Stephen smiled and helped himself to a biscuit, "She is resting now, but Doc patched her up really well and she is expected to make a full recovery. I'm going back again shortly, to stay with her."

With smiles all around, this was now a day to reflect, to celebrate and to enjoy their success.

"That is great news!" Howard said, "Please tell her that we need her to get back into shape and here with *the team* as soon as possible."

Stephen smiled then looked at Zoe and she nodded at him,

knowingly.

A little later, downstairs, in the Main Hall, Leah was singing a particularly beautiful upbeat song with Lenny and the band. Tonight, she felt strange and different; stronger, confident and aware of her newly discovered *other self*. She knew there was much more inside of her yet, and it troubled her slightly.

After the rehearsal, Leah met Shania, Mac, Taylor and Jaz in the dining area. Shania had a coffee waiting for her on their table.

"Was it a good rehearsal?" Shania asked her.

"Yes, thank you," Leah replied, sipping her coffee.

"Good!" Shania began, "Because I have some news to tell you. Mac and I are getting married, very quietly and very soon!"

"That's fabulous news!" Leah screamed and jumped up to hug them both.

Late one evening, the following week, when Mac dropped Shania home, Leah had a conversation with them both and asked Shania whether she would consider selling her, her flat. After all, Shania would be moving into Mac's stylish property just across the city after their marriage.

Leah explained, "Lincoln is my home, I knew it, the moment I first arrived here." She then informed them, "I have also made another decision, I do not plan to become a teacher, as my parents had wanted me to, I know it's not for me now."

"I am so pleased to hear you say that Leah!" Mac said excitedly, "You see, I would love to have you run the shop. You would be a great asset, identifying the *attractive* from the *important* pieces of history. I'll teach you the running of the day-to-day business, internet and private sales, etc, etc and then I will leave you to it! What do you say?"

Leah was filled with joy! "Oh yes!" she said, "I would love to!"

Soon, contracts were signed, and Leah used a part of her inheritance from Pam and William, to buy herself her own home from

Shania and a new car. She was no longer experiencing nightmares, as her *gifts* were free to reveal themselves and to be acknowledged. And she loved her new job, working for Mac in the antique business. It was the vocation she was born to do, and people were constantly amazed at her knowledge and understanding of the unusual artifacts and treasures, she bought and sold.

Leah was also becoming somewhat of an *internet sensation* with her musical talents, as her own songs performed at The Forum and streamed regularly online, were growing ever popular.

One day, Leah was about to lock-up when Zac walked into the shop. He turned the door sign to 'Closed' and approached her, standing at the counter.

"Hello *Stranger*," she said.

"Hi."

"Is that all you can say for yourself?" she asked him, "Hi?"

"You're understandably cross with me," he began, "I am sorry that I had to leave you straight after the attack at The Forum. Raama had financial and personal business I needed to sort out. I did not want to just suddenly disappear like that, but I had no choice."

Leah studied Zac for a moment, asking herself how she really *felt* about him now ... after all the things she had seen him be part of, inside of her mind.

"And have you finished *sorting out?*" she enquired.

"For now," he said, "That is what I have come to tell you. I have just bought a place to live not far from here and I was wondering whether you would be free to join me for coffee one day?"

"You have bought a place? In Lincoln?" she gasped.

"Well, I own property all around the world now," he said casually, and grinned. "Why not invest here, in Lincoln, I asked myself? Besides, Howard and my two new *besties* Taylor and Mac, want me to stay around. How would you feel about that, Leah?"

Zac searched Leah's eyes, nervously, *how would he cope if she hated and rejected him now?*

"Why not?" she smiled, shaking her head, "I suppose we can meet up for coffee regularly from now on, then? That should prove exciting, considering our past outings together."

They laughed.

The Marriage

The night before Mac and Shania's wedding, Eshan dropped Sabia home having enjoyed an evening spent together at his grandparent's home. Dharma and Zeeshan had prepared a delicious meal and they had all celebrated Eshan's relief and joy of finally 'exchanging contracts' on his own house. It had been a stressful couple of months for him, having had two previous failed attempts at buying property, but now, it was definite – he would be moving into his house in just a fortnight.

Eshan could not have been happier, especially later, when Sabia had initiated a long and passionate kiss when they had pulled up outside of her house in his car.

"I must go now. Amir has been left on his own all evening," Sabia murmured reluctantly.

Eshan had watched her walk inside the front door and wave to him, before closing it. He felt he was an *extremely lucky man indeed.*

Once inside the dark house, Sabia switched on the lights. During *the kiss*, her watch had warned her of an intruder in her home. As she had expected, she entered her lounge to discover Musad sitting on the sofa. Sat opposite him, was his nasty friend, Mike with his scarred and battered bulldog, Tyson.

As Sabia slowly entered the room, Tyson growled and choked himself with the cruel chain around his neck. She looked at the dog, then at Mike and finally at Musad.

"Welcome home, *Darling!*" he said, spitefully, whilst polishing the long blade of his knife with a tissue. Mike laughed and Tyson snarled.

Sabia turned, then slowly took a step over towards the modern sideboard unit and opened the drawer. She calmly took out a pair of white cotton gloves placed inside and carefully put them on her dainty hands.

"Stupid *bitch!*" Mike scorned.

Musad laughed, then enquired, "What are you doing Sabia?" then asked her, "And where is Amir?"

"Amir is probably taking a nap in his bedroom upstairs," Sabia replied matter-of-factly.

"He is still a pathetic *coward of a dog*, then?" he laughed.

"Ha!" Mike said, "Tyson here is going to make *mincemeat* out of him!" The men laughed. "Any way," he added, "Why is she still walking around and looking pretty, Musad? I thought you said you taught her a *right lesson* before you were kicked-out?"

With an eerily quick reaction, Sabia turned to look at Mike, "Do you like *teaching women lessons?*" she asked him.

Mike felt intimidated, looking into Sabia's cool and poised eyes. Ignorantly, he kicked Tyson into a sudden frenzy.

Hiding behind his enraged beast, he replied, "Huh! Bitches like you deserve a right kicking!"

Musad laughed out loud, "Oh, *this bitch* is getting more than a *kicking* tonight, my friend!"

As sudden as a lizard, catching an unsuspecting fly, Sabia took a step towards Musad. Swiftly and ingeniously, she took hold of the knife from his hand and through it immediately into Mike's heart.

Musad was shocked and horrified!

"What have you done?" he screamed. His lips were trembling, layers of fat wobbled as his entire body began shaking.

Mike's lifeless body, with his eyes wide open and staring right back at him, was slumped in the chair opposite. The chain restraining Tyson had slipped to the ground.

Sabia whistled to Amir, who then could be heard bounding down the stairs, having waited patiently for her command. Tyson became silent as the huge magnificent, black, long-furred dog entered the room.

In a calm confident voice, Sabia replied, "I have not done anything, Musad. It is your fingerprints on the knife, not mine. And in answer to your earlier question, Amir is doing really well nowadays, as am I. We have both ... *excelled* since you left."

Sabia made a facial command and Amir stared at Tyson, then turned his head to one side, looking rather cute for a moment.

To Musad's amazement, Tyson rolled over onto his back. Amir barked and Tyson immediately stood, then sat himself happily next to Amir.

Both dogs looked up at Sabia, then wagged their tails as she confirmed, "You are *good boys,* aren't you?"

Musad took the opportunity to attempt an escape, only to be skilfully struck by two fingers in his throat and forcefully kicked back on the sofa by his angry and violently transformed *former victim.*

He was choking as, in a voice he could never have imagined coming from his former gentle and non-offensive wife, she yelled hysterically at him, "I did not give you permission to get up!"

Musad was terrified. He felt like he was living in a scene from a poorly made, yet disturbing, horror movie.

"Please!" he cried, "Please don't hurt me!"

"Why not?" Sabia asked him coldly, "You hurt me when I asked you to stop, many, many times, but you never did. Whatever makes you think I will show *you* any mercy?"

"I'm sorry! I'm so, so sorry!" he screamed whilst still choking.

Sabia had returned from the kitchen holding a large piece of broken glass in her hand. She placed it in front of the dogs; Tyson wagged his tail and barked at Amir, Amir looked up at her and confirmed her suspicions.

"I changed the locks, so you obviously got Mike to break the window, didn't you? I suppose he is used to doing that sort of thing," Sabia stated sarcastically.

There was a small droplet of blood, close to where she had hold of the glass and she looked over at Mike's body and saw the revealing small cut on his hand.

Without warning, she suddenly sent the jagged piece of glass flying through the air, slicing into Musad's inner thigh, severing his Femoral Artery. Only the long spiked triangular tip, with Mike's blood, was visible. Musad's own blood poured out from his wound, trickled down the sofa and flowed down onto the carpet.

As Musad was dying in agony, Sabia pulled up an elegant footstall and sat directly in front of him, staring up into his face.

"That wasn't nice of Mike, was it? You should have made better choices when choosing your friends, my *darling husband*," she taunted.

When the final last agonising minute of Musad's life had left his body, Sabia replaced the perfectly clean white gloves, to the drawer and made a call. Within minutes, Robyn, a team of police officers and an ambulance crew were on the scene. Robyn made a quick call to Jaz and she and Zoe arrived shortly afterwards.

Now, Sabia was tenderly nursed by a sympathetic paramedic. Zoe sat stroking the two happy and affectionate dogs, while Jaz, stern faced, listened intently to the story Sabia told to Robyn and her colleague.

Tearfully, occasionally hysterical while convincingly suffering from the symptoms of shock, Sabia explained how Musad and Mike had broken in, intent on hurting her. She explained how Mike had suddenly demanded he have Amir, and a fight had erupted between the two friends.

"Everyone knew how much Musad cared for Amir, from how he showed it at our wedding! He loved that dog more than anything!" she had cried innocently.

The bodies of Musad and Mike were carried away in body bags. Evidence had been collected from the crime scene, though it was *obvious that the men, with documented histories of violence, had* fought and *killed one another.*

Having reassured Robyn and the other members of the Emergency Services that she did not require, nor want, further medical attention, she was left alone with Zoe, Jaz and the dogs.

"Come back home with me tonight, Sabia," Zoe suggested, "You don't want to be surrounded by all of this," she said, looking down at the blood on the carpet.

"I will be fine," Sabia said brightly, "Besides, we've all got a wedding to attend tomorrow."

Zoe stood up and walked into the kitchen, "I will just clear this glass away, we don't want the dogs treading on it, do we?"

Sabia looked at Jaz, who was staring back at her.

Jaz hesitated, then spoke softly, "You know you can't use your ... *skills*, for your own personal wars."

Sabia did not change her expression.

"I have just saved countless other women from suffering the same abuse that I did," she whispered back, vehemently and proudly, "I have no regrets and would do it all again."

At that moment, Zoe returned to the lounge, bringing with her a mug of sweet tea she had prepared after clearing up the broken glass at the backdoor window.

"Are you sure you will be okay now?" she asked, placing the hot mug carefully into Sabia's calm hands.

Sabia smiled and looked down at the dogs as they came and sat protectively at her feet.

"I will be perfectly fine now. Thank you," she said.

As Jaz and Zoe left the house and headed for their cars parked outside, Jaz was seriously concerned that Sabia could prove to be a huge problem in the future.

She spoke quietly to Zoe, "You know she did it, don't you?"

"Of course, she did it," Zoe replied casually.

"But it was wrong!" Jaz exclaimed, shocked at Zoe's cool response.

"Oh, I don't know," Zoe continued, smiling, "I think I should suggest to Howard that Sabia should work alongside Shania, supporting our Domestic Abuse Victims. I think she'd be great at it!"

Jaz was left standing dumbfounded, wondering whether Zoe was serious or not, as she watched her get into her car, then wave happily at her before driving away.

The following morning, when Jaz and Robyn were getting dressed for Mac and Shania's Wedding, Jaz would remain silent as Rob spoke of the, *'Poor Sabia',*

"... but how good things have turned out because she will inherit all of her abuser's assets, as they weren't yet divorced, and she will be rid of him forever!'

The Wedding Day

The weather was beautiful as the morning sunshine smiled down upon the small chapel on the Kingstone Estate.

Gemma, Leah and Taylor had assisted Maria in decorating it with flowers and various colourful woodland garlands the previous evening. Inside it smelt as beautiful as it looked. The boarded-up windows now lit up as the sunlight streamed through the ancient stained glass and the newly polished pulpit, baring Howard's Bible, added to the ancient and spiritual atmosphere.

The bride looked radiant, dressed in a plain, full-sleeved, long silk white dress. Her hair was piled in soft golden curls upon her head and decorated with delicate flowers that matched her natural and sweet-smelling bouquet.

Leah, her Maid of Honour, wore the same style dress as Shania, but in the colour of soft peach, and her shiny dark hair remained down. Leah could easily have been the perfect bride herself.

Mac was as handsome as a groom possibly could be. His tall muscular body looked perfect in an expensive black suit, white shirt and colourful tie. Taylor, his best friend and Groom was dressed exactly the same as Mac, looking as equally attractive.

The Wedding Procession walked past the guests stood outside of the chapel. Stephen and Gemma, Jaz and Robyn, Mahdi, Rafi, Eshan and Sabia with Amir and Tyson by her side, could clearly hear the words spoken by Howard, performing the short but meaningful ceremony. Only George, Maria and Zoe were seated inside, on the decorated benches.

Afterwards, the Wedding Party returned to the Kingstone Manor House, where a large marquee had been erected on the lawn of the enormous back garden. Professional caterers prepared and served delicious food throughout the enjoyable day as a few more invited guests arrived to enjoy the celebrations. They included Benjamin, looking smart in his chosen red spotted bowtie, accompanied by his parents and younger sister and the elderly caretaker of Temple Bruer.

Later, Leah was dancing with Taylor when she noticed Zac had arrived and was speaking to Howard. She watched as Maria joined their conversation and smiled as she considered how *ordinary* and *normal*, it all appeared to an outsider.

Zac then went over to congratulate Mac and Shania, shaking the groom's hand and kissing the cheek of the smiling bride.

Leah watched as Maria was approached by Sabia, who introduced her to Tyson. It was clearly *love at first sight* and the poor creature, who had suffered an existence of neglect and brutality at the hands of Mike, was to begin his new happier and thoroughly spoilt life, as one of Maria's *puppies*. He would be welcomed into *the pack* and eventually given the *gift of eternal life* by its alpha, named Zeus.

When Zac had finished speaking to Mac and Shania, he turned and caught sight of Leah, his heart ached, for she looked so beautiful.

He would give up everything to have just one day on this Earth, as her husband.

Their eyes met. Just as Zac was imagining holding her in his arms, Taylor noticed him and led Leah straight over to where he was standing.

"It's good to see you here!" Taylor said warmly.

"It's good to see you too, Taylor," Zac replied genuinely.

Before anything else could be said, the music suddenly became louder as a lively but sensual Latin song replaced the romantic ballad.

Everyone rushed to the dance floor and Maria grabbed hold of Zac's hand, "Come and dance with me, Zachariah!" she said, dragging him on to the dance floor.

George, who was sitting at a table, close by, called out to him, "There is no good in refusing that woman anything!" he laughed.

Taylor smiled at Leah and offered her his hand, as Shania and Mac whizzed past them, racing to get to the dancefloor.

"Shall we show them all how it's done?" he asked.

"Absolutely!" Leah replied joyfully.

This was a day of celebration. A day to celebrate love, friendship, commitment and loyalty. It would be remembered as a special and wonderful time and all there would cherish this memory always.

Life is a roller coaster ...

A few weeks later, Leah was handed an *artifact* by a new client, wanting her to value a silver chalice. The woman said she had discovered it beneath the floorboards of an old house that she and her husband had recently bought and had begun to refurbish.

As Leah held the chalice, flashes of light and wild images filled her head. Long forgotten memories of her mother's murder began to resurface. Then she saw the face of her aunt again, only looking older this time. Grace was performing a *dark ceremony*, surrounded by a circle of demons and dark witches.

Leah recognised Sybil amongst the group. She heard and understood the words Grace called out in anguish, "I will revenge you, Raama, *My Love!*"

Next, she saw the face of a dark-skinned middle-aged man with surprisingly bright blue eyes and long grey plaited dreadlocks. She *felt* she knew him, that she *loved* him, and he *loved* her. His surroundings looked tropical. Sat crossed legged on the golden sand, he looked out towards the vast blue ocean and spoke as though he was talking directly to her.

"Be careful, Leah! She must be stopped!" he said purposefully.

"Excuse me! Are you okay?" the woman asked again.

Leah returned to consciousness, "Yes, sorry, I'm fine. Er, ... please, come this way and I can show you what your chalice is worth and what I am prepared to pay you for it."

The woman left the shop a few minutes later, well satisfied with her payment.

Leah immediately placed her, *'Back at 2 pm'* sign on the door and closed the shop.

Taking her phone from out of her bag, Leah called Howard, "Hi Howard," she said, "I hope I'm not disturbing you in the middle of anything important, but ... I'm afraid to tell you that ... we've more trouble ahead."

Zoe looked dubiously across the kitchen table at her husband. The happy expression upon his face had completely changed on answering his phone.

"Thank you, Leah," he said, the colour now draining from his face, "When you have finished rehearsals tonight with the band, could you please pop upstairs and join us all for a meeting? You had better fill us all in together."

Zoe was concerned. As Howard put down his phone, she asked, "So, what is wrong?"

Howard's reply was calm and cool, as he lifted his mug of tea towards his mouth, "Well," he said, pushing his plate away, "That news has just completely taken the joy out of my chocolate biscuits."

Meanwhile, across the city, Leah had just met up with Zac for coffee at their usual outside café. As she joined him at their table, both their phones made the same sound at the exact same time.

They looked at their phones and read the group-message that had just been sent by Taylor.

"So," Zac said smiling up at Leah, "I guess our lives just got exciting again?"

Leah smiled back at him, and replied, "When were the lives of knights, demons and witches *ever* **not** exciting?"

Suddenly, Leah's phone lit up again and made another sound. Taylor had just sent her a line of kisses which Zac had seen.

She smiled as Zac muttered, "*Bible Boy* doesn't give up, does he?"

"You're just upset that he didn't send you any kisses!" she joked. They both laughed and enjoyed their coffee.

The End

ACKNOWLEDGEMENT

Thank Heaven for historical and magical places such as Temple Bruer. May they forever inspire us to use our imagination and to ask questions like ... what if?

Dee Horne

ABOUT THE AUTHOR

Dee Horne

Born in Essex, my husband and I moved our young family to Lincolnshire in 2000. We love it here and my interest in history, music and different religious beliefs helped me to create my first novel. I enjoy visiting historical places and allowing my imagination to run wild by touching walls, asking myself, who else throughout history might have stood within them?
After visiting Temple Bruer, I felt inspired to write a fictional story about this incredible place. I completed it during the first lockdown in 2020.

I love creating characters with difficult pasts who overcome their challenges and the expectations of others to become successful and likeable people. More secrets of my characters will be revealed in the continuing short stories from Temple Bruer. The first being, 'Shania and the Boy of Gold' (2021)

I hope you will enjoy reading them as much as I have enjoyed writing them!

FUTURE TALES FROM THE KNIGHTS OF TEMPLE BRUER

Coming Next ...

Shania And The Boy Of Gold

Printed in Great Britain
by Amazon